OOOOOH, I AM SO EXCITED MY LEGS ARE WIGGLING AROUND FOR no reason. They are uncontrollable. They might calm down when I shove them in my boots.

I feel soooo lucky to be here. It feels great to have proper friends and to be on the brink of being a showbiz legend. Or, well, being on the course.

I know it's childish but I wanted to dance and sing with pleasure. I only wish I could do either.

Anything goes in the crazy world of theater, dahling. I might be discovered and asked to be Maria in *The Sound of Music* in the West End. That would make Alex know I was proper girlfriend material, and not some little girl with nobbly knees.

Also by Louise Rennison

The (Mis)Adventures of Tallulah Casey books:

WITHERING TIGHTS

The Confessions of Georgia Nicolson books:

ANGUS, THONGS AND FULL-FRONTAL SNOGGING

ON THE BRIGHT SIDE, I'M NOW THE GIRLFRIEND OF A SEX GOD

KNOCKED OUT BY MY NUNGA-NUNGAS

DANCING IN MY NUDDY-PANTS

AWAY LAUGHING ON A FAST CAMEL

THEN HE ATE MY BOY ENTRANCERS

STARTLED BY HIS FURRY SHORTS

LOVE IS A MANY TROUSERED THING

STOP IN THE NAME OF PANTS!

ARE THESE MY BASOOMAS I SEE BEFORE ME?

A MiDSUMMER TiGHTS DREAM

Louise Rennison

HARPER TEEN
An Imprint of HarperCollinsPublishers

HarperTeen is an imprint of HarperCollins Publishers.

A Midsummer Tights Dream

 For information address HarperCollins Children's Books, a division of HarperCollins Publishers, 10 East 53rd Street, New York, NY 10022.
www.epicreads.com

Library of Congress catalog card number: 2012935601
ISBN 978-0-06-179938-9 (pbk.)

Typography by Becky Terhune
13 14 15 16 17 LP/RRDH 10 9 8 7 6 5 4 3 2 1
❖
First paperback edition, 2013

Big love to all my fabby mates and family. A special thanks this time to my groovy little sister and mum, who read everything and also wouldn't allow the hilarious Cain "dead rabbit crying" scene at the end, which I will never tell a soul about. But it would've been very, very funny for the rabbit to have pretended to be crying, I think.

P. S. Gillie, Lizzie, Clare, and Cassie, and all the lovely peeps at Aitken Alexander and HarperCollins (including the god-like Gillon Aitken), I'm really sorry for not going away—and staring out from the boardroom, day after day, like a big cuckoo in your office.

Big kiss to Jo and Matilda, hoofys all round.

Contents

Back on the showbiz express

Performing Arts College, here I come again! Hold on to your tights! Because I am holding on to mine, I can tell you. Which makes it difficult to go to the loo, but that is the price of fame. And fame is my game!

Once more I am chugging back to Dother Hall. Or "the theater of dreams," as Sidone Beaver, the principal, calls it. I am truly on the showbiz express of life.

Well, the stopping train to Skipley, the Entertainment Capital of the North. Or home of the West Riding Otter, as some not-showbiz people call it. (I don't think they mean that only a big fat otter lives in the town, although you never know!)

Hooray and chug-a-lug-a-doo-dah!!!

I feel like shouting out to the heavens. I think I will.

I can now because the grumpy woman with the stick got off at the last stop. Oh, the Northern folk with their jolly Northern ways. She was so grumpy about her gammy leg. She said the stick had worn down on one side so that she fell over in strong winds. I didn't ask her any of this—she just told me. But hey-nonny-no, as Shakespeare said. I am going to pull down the window and shout out loud:

"The name is Tallulah. Tallulah Casey!!! And I'm back. I'm moving up! Moving on up! Nothing can stop me! Yes, I used to be shy and gangly with nobbly knees and no sticky-out bits. No corkers. I was corkerless. I didn't even wear a corker holder. But now even my corkers are on the move!"

Especially when the train keeps stopping unexpectedly. What now? Maybe the West Riding Otter is on the line. The tannoy is crackling but I can only hear heavy breathing and snuffling. Lawks a mercy, the wild otter has hijacked the train!

I don't care about the otter driver! Live and let live, I say.

Uh-oh, the tannoy is crackling again.

"Sorry about that, ladies and gentlemen, I momentarily lost hold of my pie. Next stop Skipley."

We're just passing Grimbottom Peak. Brr. It looks so dark and forbidding up there on the crags. I'm surprised it's not pouring down with rain and . . . It is pouring down with rain.

Crumbs, it's like the lights have been turned off. You can hardly see Grimbottom. The locals say that when day-trippers are up there the fog can come down in minutes. Mr. Bottomly at the post office once told me and Flossie:

"One minute t'day-trippers are up there on't top, playing piggy in't middle like barm pots. The next it's so dark they can't even see t'ball. And it's in their hand. Hours later the grown-ups stumble home but the little'uns are nivver seen no more.

"Sometimes late at night tha can hear 'em up there wailing, 'Mummeee . . . Dadeeeee . . .' All them lost bairns, speaking from beyond the grave."

Flossie had said to Mr. Bottomly, "That's rubbish. I think there's a massive wild dog up there called Fang. Half dog, half donkey, and it comes out in the fog and takes the children and raises them as its puppies."

In my opinion, even though I haven't known her for long, my new friend Flossie is what is commonly known as "mad."

But mad or not, I am really, really excited about seeing her and my new mates again. Vaisey and Flossie and little Jo and Honey, who can't say her "r"s but knows everything about boys. She says she always has "two or thwee on the go."

We can go into the woods near Dother Hall again, to our special place! And gather round our special tree. Our special tree where we met the boys from Woolfe Academy when they surprised us doing our special dance that Honey taught us. She said we had to be proud of all of ourselves, even the bits we didn't like. It was a "showing our inner glory" dance. Or "inner glowee" as Honey called it. Which in my case was hurling my legs around shouting, "I love my knees, I love them!"

Not quite as embarrassing as Vaisey waggling her bottom at the tree, but close.

The Woolfe Academy boys, well, Charlie and Phil, call us the "Tree Sisters."

Charlie said to me . . .

Well, I won't think about Charlie. Not after what happened after he kissed me.

Where was I in my performing life? Oh yes, last summer when I got to Dother Hall I couldn't do anything. The others could sing and dance and act, but all I could do was be tall and do a bit of Irish dancing.

I was convinced that I would never be asked back and that I would never wear the golden slippers of applause. Things changed when Blaise Fox, the dance tutor, saw my Sugar Plum Bikey performance. My ballet based on the Sugar Plum Fairy—only done on a bicycle. The one when my ballet skirt got caught in the back wheel, and I accidentally shot off my bike and destroyed the backstage area. I remember what she said.

She said: "Tallulah Casey, watching you is like watching someone whose pants are on fire." Then she asked me to play Heathcliff in *Wuthering Heights* at the end of last term. And the rest is showbiz legend.

Heathcliff's Irish-dancing solo was a triumph! And, also, not so easy in tight trousers.

I still don't know why she cast me as Heathcliff though.

Perhaps I really do look like a boy?

If I look down and squint my eyes a bit, I can definitely see pimply bumps in the corker area.

No one can argue with that. The front of a jumper never lies.

My jumper is one of the ones Cousin Georgia and her Ace Gang chose for me. It's green and she says it goes with my eyes and gives me je ne sais quoi.

Well, she actually said, "It says 'ummmmmmm' but not 'oooohhhh, look at me, I'm a tart.'"

I can't wait to get to Skipley. I'm so excited. This is going to be my Winter of Love, I can tell.

I stayed with Cousin Georgia on my way back from summer school and it was brilliant. I haven't really spent a lot of time with her before because of being in Ireland and having crap parents who actually do stuff. Not just bake tarts or DIY like everyone else's parents. Not good old boring stuff. My mum goes off and paints and my dad goes off exploring to find endangered things. He collects mollusks mostly but last time he found a rare hairy potato. He's like a cross between David Bellamy and . . . a Labrador. That is not a proper dad in anyone's language.

That's a Labradad.

Hee. I think that might very nearly be a joke.

I'm going to put it into my performance-art notebook that I will be keeping.

I've got a special new notebook with a black glossy cover and some plums on the front of it.

It's really arty, and er . . . fruity.

I've already made my first entry.

It says:

Winter of Love.

I'll just add my "Labradad" idea.

Labradad. A portrait of a dad who is half pipe-smoking bloke and half Labrador. He's confused between the two worlds. Between pipes and sticks. I'm thinking an improvised dance piece. Perhaps the Labradad fetching sticks. Or pipes?

Or ducks?

Hmmmmm.

I love my parents but they're not normal. Or around much. But they have let me come back to Dother Hall—even though I have to stay with the Dobbinses. My mum said I was too immature to board but she doesn't seem to mind that I'm staying with a family where the mother is a Brown Owl and the father goes to "inner woman" groups. Which is not to mention the idiot twins.

It was great staying with Cousin Georgia. It was brilliant on the boy front as well.

She got her Ace Gang round to teach me "wisdomosity" and also "snogging techniques." We all tucked up in her bed, which was cozy.

Georgia said, "Have a jammy dodger and give us the goss snogwise."

The Ace Gang were wearing false beards to help me get into the mood.

So . . . I told them about going to the cinema in Skipley with some boys from Woolfe Academy and about my first kiss. With floppy Ben. And how it was like having a little bat trapped in my mouth.

The Ace Gang looked at me and Georgia said, "Tallulah, are you a fool with just a hint of an idiot thrown in?"

But they gave me their wisdomosity about boys. And snogging.

Gosh, Georgia knows a lot.

About varying pressure of the lips, what to do with your tongue (don't waggle it about like a fool), the scoring system for snogging. (Number 1 to Number 10, I can't remember all of them but I do remember Number 4 is "a kiss lasting over three minutes without a break." You need a mate for that one, so that they can time it for you.)

Honestly. I couldn't believe it.

I'm dying to try out my new skills.

The amount she knew, she must have spent all of her time doing snogging research.

I said that to her and she said, "I do, my strange gangly cousy. But I have put aside snogging to teach you the ways of boydom. I do it because I luuurve you. But not in a lezzie way."

Which is good.

I think.

What is a "lezzie way"?

I think it's to do with girl snogging.

But I didn't ask.

Oh chuggy-chug-chug. Come on, train!!!

I wonder what time the rest of the Tree Sisters will arrive tomorrow?

Oh, here we are at the train station. Hurrah!!! There's its sign swinging in the biting gale force wind. Just as I remember:

Skipley
Home of the
West Riding Otter

Hang on a minute, some Northern vandal has painted

a "b" and a "y" over the otter bit. So now it reads:

Well, here I am, back where I really belong. I have just got off the showbiz express and crossed to the other side of the station and now I am getting on the bus of hope. Which will transport me to . . . The Theater of Dreams.

I can see the bus driver through the closed door, sitting in the driver's seat. I recognize him from last term. I wonder if he recognizes me?

As I hauled my bag on board up the steps he put the pipe to one side of his mouth and shouted, "Stop messing about and get on if you're getting on, merry legs. It's bloody parky with that door open."

I said, "Why did you call me merry legs?"

He said, “Because you’re lanky and your legs are all over the shop.”

As I paid my fare he said, “Come back to prat around like a fool at Dither Hall again, have you?”

Before I could say “It’s Dother Hall, actual—” he accelerated off so violently that I shot down to the end of the bus and almost ended up in a small child’s pushchair. Luckily there wasn’t a small child in it, just a pig.

The woman with the pushchair said, “Mind my pig.”

I am huddled up well away from her, but I think I can still smell pig poo.

We bumped along the road to Heckmondwhite. The driver is careering along sounding his horn whenever there is anything in his way on the road. Pedestrians. Bicyclists. A cow pat. But he slowed down behind a lollipop lady who was walking home. With her sign. She tried to let him pass but he cheerily waved her on and drove slowly behind her. Then for no reason when we got to a sharp corner he revved up and blasted his horn and she fell into a hedge. He was laughing so much I thought he might swallow his pipe.

I couldn’t help being excited. This is like a postcard of a winter scene in Yorkshire. There is even some snow on the top of Grimbottom Peak. And I shivered as I thought about Fang up there. Raising his fictitious children as fictitious puppies.

Winter of Love

AS THE SKY DARKENED and we bumped past isolated farms and little hamlets, we arrived at the bus stop in Heckmondwhite just when the street lamps were lighting up. In my Dother Hall brochure it says, "Heckmondwhite has its own 'zany' cosmopolitan atmosphere."

I don't know that most people would call a village green and a post office and a pub called The Blind Pig "zany." Unless you counted the knitted flags over the village hall.

I bet the Dobbinses, my substitute parents, have got something to do with that.

Maybe I should just nip quickly over to the pub and see my fun-sized friend, Ruby, and my four-legged mate Matilda, her bulldog? I could give her the lipstick I've bought her. Not Matilda, Ruby. Dogs don't wear makeup. But what they do wear is the little ballet tutu I have got for her from Pets Party shop. I hope it will go round her waist. She is quite porky in the middle.

And anyway, even if Rubes is out I could leave the presents with her older brother, Alex. Alex the dream boy. Alex with his long limbs and his longish thick chestnut hair. And his two eyes. And his back and front . . . and everything. And we could chat about performing arts. He's gone off to Liverpool to do drama there and I could chat about my performance plans. Maybe tell him about my Labradad idea.

Maybe not. I want him to think of me as an attractive thespian.

Yes, I will pop to see Ruby. And whilst I am popping about maybe Alex, her very gorgeous brother, will pop up and that will be poptastic and I will say, "What a surprise, Alex, I was just popping by to . . ."

"Lullah! Lullah, yoo-hoo, it's me!!!! And the twins!!!"

Dibdobs. In her Brown Owl uniform, coming toward me. No, not just coming toward me. Skipping toward me.

The twins were wearing knitted yellow knickerbockers.

I bet Mr. Dobbins (Harold) knitted them at one of his "inner woman" groups. Harold goes to a men's group and they try to find their hidden feminine side.

Uuuumph. She almost crushed me to death with her bosom and her badges. And her new whistle. As I have said before, I am sure Dibdobs has got a "hugging" badge. She's got badges for everything else, moth conservation, vole watching, pond life, etc.

I couldn't actually see anything when she was hugging me, but I could feel hugging going on around my knee area as well.

That would be the twins, Max and Sam.

They love my knees.

Probably because that is as far up as their toddler arms can hug.

I don't get a lot of hugging at home.

My little brother, Connor, likes kicking mostly. I hugged him when I left and he said, "Don't be so gay." Grandma does a lot of patting. But quite often she's off target with that and thinks she is patting me when actually it's the cushion next to me.

Dibdobs was talking really loudly and quickly like she does. She's so keen on everything.

It's nice really. Just odd.

"Oh, Lullah, it's sooooooo lovely to have you back. I've missed you. We've all missed you. Haven't we, boys?"

The boys stood there blinking from underneath their pudding basin haircuts.

And sucking their dodies.

They don't get any less odd.

Dibdobs said, "The boys have made something for you. Haven't you, boys?"

She adores the twins. She thinks they are covering up their cleverness. She thinks they are like tiny little brain surgeons in tiny twits' clothing.

Max and Sam blinked at me. And kept on sucking.

Then Max (or Sam) took his dodie out and said, "Sjuuuuge one for ooo."

I said, "Oh, well, that's nice, I . . ."

Dibdobs said, "Tell Lullah what you've made for her."

Sam said, "Sjuuuuge."

Dibdobs started slightly losing her rag. "Yes, yes, it is quite big . . . but TELL Lullah what it is."

Sam blinked and looked a bit cross, like he had suddenly realized he had a Brown Owl for a mother. He put his hands on his hips and stamped his foot and said, "SJJJJUUUUGE."

And Max shouted, "BOGIES!!!"

Dibdobs went even redder.

She bent down so she could look them both in the eyes and said sternly, "Now, that is a silly, silly word that big boys don't say anymore."

Max and Sam blinked together and smiled. Great Jumping Jehovah, they look like sock animals when they smile.

Dibdobs took their hands and we all walked back to the house. She was chatting on sixteen to the dozen. But I could still hear Max and Sam softly singing, "Bogie, bogie, bogie, bogie, bogie."

Dibdobs said, "Harold is so looking forward to seeing

you. He's out tonight with the interknitting group. After the success of the communal skipping rope, you know, the skipathon when the whole village skipped?"

Oh yes, I remembered that.

She was chattering on.

"Well, he's got big plans for knitting the village together for Christmas. Won't that be fun?"

I don't know what to say to that because she hugged me again and my mouth was in her muffler.

When we got back to Dandelion Cottage the twins' present turned out to be some bits of feather stuck into a potato.

Max said, "Fevver man for ooo."

Lovely.

Also there was a postcard addressed to me care of the Dobbinses. It was from Honey! It just said:

Dear Tallulah,

Something WEALLY exciting has happened!!!! See you when I get there on Wednesday and tell you all about it!!!

Honey xxx

It didn't really say "weally" on the postcard, but I could hear her voice in my head.

I wonder what she means?

Maybe she's got five boyfriends now?!

I took my luggage (and "Fevver man") up into my room while Dibdobs went to make some tea.

So here I am back in my old squirrel room. Sitting on my wooden bed with the squirrel carved into the bedhead. With my feather potato. I've brought back my squirrel slippers, the ones that Dibdobs gave me when I first came. She said they were to make me feel at home.

Which they would have done, had my home been in an oak tree.

I put the squirrel slippers into the bed for company. Well, one looks like a squirrel and the other one looks like a hamster. My brother, Connor, set fire to one of the tail bits so it's just a stump.

I looked around at the familiar carved wooden wardrobe (acorn theme) and the wooden dressing table (with the carved squirrel legs) and the wooden, well, everything really. You name it, if it was in the room, it was wooden.

But wood was OK. Everything was OK.

I put my case on the bed and started to unpack. Georgia and her Ace Gang helped me choose cool things to suit my shape. Like dark tights and bright little skirts. And hats. The Ace Gang said I needed to de-emphasize my bad bits (nobbly knees) and emphasize my good bits (catty eyes and nice swishy black hair). Georgia said to distract boys from my knee area I should swish my hair almost constantly. (Although not to fiddle with my fringe, because she personally thought that was a killing offense.)

I hung all my stuff in the wooden wardrobe.

I even have a special underwear drawer. With bras in it. Oh yes!

Yes, I now officially wear corker holders.

And what's more, I have corkers to put in them!!

I've got the tiniest corker appliances you can get (30A), but I have high hopes for a growth spurt when I start tap-dancing my way to the top of the showbiz ladder. Not that I can tap-dance, but I could do something on the ladder, I'm sure. It's just a question of finding it and not falling off the ladder in the meantime. Even though you can't see the ladder.

Ooh, it will be so nice to see little Vaisey again and her cheeky bottom and all my new arty mates.

I'm putting my new shiny, fruity performance-art notebook under my pillow for when I come up with more whizzo creative projects. I can't wait to see Dr. Lightowler's face when she has to hand me my golden slippers of applause.

She doesn't like me. I don't know why. It was after I did my "owl-laying-an-egg" mime in her class. I think she took against me then.

Maybe she thought I was pretending to be her because

she looks like an owl. She said I was silly and shouldn't be at Dother Hall.

But Dr. Owly is in for a surprise when she gets to see how unsilly I can be.

I'm going to put my corker-measuring tape measure in my corker-holder drawer, next to my corker holders.

I wonder if my corkers have grown since I last measured them?

I did a sneaky measuring in the lavatory on the train, which is only about three hours ago, but growing could happen any time, couldn't it?

It could happen the minute after you took the corker-measuring tape measure away.

Anyway, I am not going to risk doing a measure. It would be just my luck for the lunatic twins to come barging in.

Last term, unfortunately I tried my method in front of the window. And Cain Hinchcliff was out there in the undergrowth, snogging some village girl, and he'd seen me, seen me doing my method. He'd seen me rubbing my corkers with my hiking socks on my hands.

To make them grow.

My corkers, not the socks.

The socks were huge.

Best not to think about it.

I shivered at the memory.

Still, that was all in the past.

Dibdobs shouted up, "Tea's ready! Boys! Tallulah! Split splat!!!"

I shook my hair and gave it a bit of a va-va-voom.

When I opened my door, there they were. The twins. Blinking and sucking on their dodies. As if they knew that I had nearly measured my corkers.

Perhaps they have a corker-sensing gene.

Perhaps all boys do.

What a horrific thought.

After tea (local eggs and a local sausage), I said, "I'm just going to pop to The Blind Pig to see Ruby and then we might pop and visit the owlets."

I've entered the "popping zone" again. I like it. It's very me.

As I went out the door Dibdobs said, "Put this hat on in case of rain. It's my camping hat."

I said, "I'll be all ri—"

But she was ramming the waterproof hat on my head, completely squashing my va-va-voomed hair. I'd have to not take it off now in case of hat hair.

Dobbins said, "Oooooh, look at you!! You're gorgeous. You've grown! Oooohhhhh."

And she hugged me again.

And so did the boys.

It's very hard to walk when you've got three people doing hugging.

Was it going to happen every time I went out?

Maybe the right thing to do was to hug them back and then they would let me go.

But that made it worse.

Dibdobs started hugging more tightly and I think she might have been crying.

I got away at last by saying, "Bye then!!!"

I was only going three feet across the green. What if we went on a school trip?

The sign (a pig in dark glasses with a white stick) was creaking in the cold wind.

I remembered last sitting here.

On the wall next to the pub.

With Alex.

Dreamy Alex.

He'd looked at me and smiled his smile. It was the best moment of my life so far. We were so close. I wanted to say so much. I wanted my eyes to speak the words I couldn't say. (Which actually might have been a bit of a surprise to both of us if they had done.)

So I had said to him, "My knees are too far up."

Why?

Why would you say that?

And then he had wanted to look at my knees to see how far up they were, and the whole thing had gone wrong, leaving him thinking I was just a stupid little kid.

With out-of-control legs.

Well, I will not be saying that sort of thing to him again.

In fact I'm going to make a "normal" list in my performance-art notebook.

Topics that a normal person would talk about.

Topics that are not knee-based.

Like theater.

Yes, yes, I will tell him about the plays I have seen.

Well, actually I haven't seen any plays.

Books, then. Yes, books.

I could say, "That Dickens writes a lot, doesn't he?"

Ruby came bursting out of the pub door.

"I saw you through the winder. Ullo ullo. It's me!!! And Matilda!!!"

Matilda was barking and throwing herself at me, jumping up. Well, sort of. She was just thudding against my calves to be fair. Her bulldoggy face looks like she is doing a turned-down squashy smile all the time. Maybe she is.

Ruby was laughing and her pigtails were jiggling about like ears underneath her hat.

She was still yelling, "Ullo ullo!!!"

It was so nice to see her little freckly face and gappy teeth.

She was skipping around me and shouting, "She's

back, she's back!!! Matilda, show Loobylullah how tha can die for England!"

Matilda stopped leaping and lay on her back with her stumpy bow legs in the air.

Ruby said, "Do your Irish dancing over her. She likes that. Go on. I'll do the singing. 'Hiddly diddly diddly. Hiddly diddly diddly.'"

As she was bobbing around she said, "You should see the owlets! Shall we go for a wander now? You'll not believe it. They've got right fat. Come on, come on."

As she went skipping off, I said, "Should you tell your dad where you're going? Or . . . or . . . Alex?"

She shouted back, "He's not in. He's forming a heavy metal band in Ormskirk."

What?

I caught up with her crossing the green.

I said, "Alex has formed a heavy metal band in Ormskirk? But—"

She said, "Not Alex, tha barm pot. Alex has gone off t'college. Me dad. You should see him in his band stuff. He's got these right tight leather trousers. It's horrible, and sometimes he can't get them off. Or walk up stairs in them."

As we went down by the side of the sheep field, I said, "I didn't even know your dad could play a guitar."

"Believe me—he can't—but he can shout bloody loud and he's got his own Viking helmet. It's a tribute band."

I said, "What to? Vikings?"

And she said, "No, it's a tribute band to pies. They're called 'The Iron Pies.'"

I hope I never have to see them.

So no Alex around then.

I sighed.

No Mr. Darcy to look at and try out my new boy skills on.

As we walked along I said, "Rubes, do you think my knees have got less nobblier?"

Ruby stopped hopping and looked at them. Then she bent down and knocked my knee with her fist. Quite hard. I said, "Owww."

She said, "Aye, I think they av a bit."

Then she looked up at me.

"I tell thee what, that corker rubbing has worked a bit too. Tha looks like you've got two walnuts down your jumper. You haven't, have you?"

I tried not to smirk. Walnuts now but maybe coconuts soon.

We were passing by the back of the Dobbinses' house. It seemed so familiar to be back here, but so much had changed. I was a woman now with womanly bits. And womanly bits' holders. In various colors.

Ruby said, "Ay up, what did tha mean in your letter? You know, you said you would tell me abaht Charlie when you saw me. Yes, you thought he thought you were a long lanky twit and that, didn't you?"

I said, "Er, Ruby. No, I didn't think he thought I was a long lanky twit, actually. I'm not a long lanky tw—"

At which point I caught my head a glancing blow on a low-lying branch.

Ruby tried not to laugh. I rubbed my head as we walked on through the dark woods and crouched a bit.

Ruby said, "Go on then."

I wasn't her plaything. I was a sensitive human being. I said, "I think you're too young . . . I don't think you'd understand."

She said, "Well, I understood about Ben, when you said kissing him were like having a little bat trapped in your mouth."

She was going on, toddling around in front of me.

"Some boys are so useless at snogging. I don't know why they don't practice before they come bothering you. They could practice on . . . balloons or, or potatoes or a . . . melon or summat."

Balloons? There was a whole world of snogging I knew nothing about and Ruby was only eleven.

Actually, it was making me feel sad thinking about Charlie. I'd really liked him. He made me laugh. And I thought he sort of liked me.

We were at the barn by now. I wanted to make sure that Connie had gone off. I said to Rube, "I don't want my head pecked off by an enormous angry barn owl. It's not even as though she would peck it off at once and get it over and done with. I saw her eat a mouse, head first, bit by bit. Till only its tail was hanging out of her beak."

So Ruby crept off and opened the barn door while I crouched behind a bush.

I noticed Matilda sat down behind me. Clearly she didn't want her head pecked off either.

Ruby came back skipping and said, "They're on their own, come in!!!"

I went into the barn and when my eyes adjusted to the dark I could see them. Little Ruby and Little Lullah. Our little owlets.

Little owlets? They were HUGE! We spent an hour with the furry freaks. They can flutter about now, although they do crash into the walls. And they swooped down onto our hats. I think they love us and think we are their stupid friends who don't even know how to fly. Well, maybe I can't fly but I don't poo myself all the time. I said to Ruby, "Look, they are pooing while they are eating."

Ruby said, "Ah know, sometimes you can see little mouse claws in the poo pellets."

It was getting cold and late, so Ruby put them back on their hay pile. I didn't want to handle them in case I was involved in a poo situation. But they were so sweet and they fluffed their feathers up to make themselves look bigger. And did head swiveling, to show off how far they could swivel. I feel proud of them.

I said to Ruby as we left them, cheeping away in the dark, "Little Lullah looks like me, don't you think?"

As she pulled her hat down she said, "Don't make me have to go say owt to me dad about you saying an owlet looks like you."

It was spooky down the dark lane with the noises in the fields and the rain and moaning wind. There were strange rustlings in the trees and a far-off hooting.

Ruby huddled into her jacket and threw a stick for Matilda. Matilda looked at the stick as it flew over her head. Then she just went on toddling along. She knows that it's not a biscuit, so why would she bother to go and get it?

Ruby said, "The Hinchcliffs have had a reight big fight. They smashed the Bottomlys' outdoor lavatory when they fell into it."

I tutted.

Typical.

"What were they fighting about this time? Who was the stupidest?"

Ruby said, "No, Ruben found out that Cain had been laiking around with his girlfriend."

I tutted again.

Ruby went on. "Cain made it worse by saying he was only doing Ruben a favor because she was a real mardy bum. And thick."

Charming.

As we got back to the Dobbinses' gate Ruby said, "Oh, I forgot, Alex gi' me a letter for thee but I left it in my room. I'll gi' it thee tomorrow."

I tried not to leap in the air or do Irish dancing. I said, "Oh, well. You know I had better . . . er, walk you to your door because of the . . . night . . . er, stuff."

Ruby rolled her eyes at me. "Come on then, soft lass."

We went across the green to The Blind Pig and Ruby ran up the back stairs to her room.

I was hovering around by the door. With a bit of luck, I wouldn't have to bump into Ted . . . at which point Ted Barraclough, Ruby's dad, came out of the front bar.

I couldn't help noticing he had a Viking helmet on.

And a guitar in his hand.

And was wearing a very tight pair of leather trousers. He was walking with small steps.

His whole big face lit up when he saw me. Oh dear.

"Well, what a lovely surprise—the thespian is back at last. Thank the Lord. Now then. Don't tell me, let me guess what you are pretending to be this time."

I said politely, "Hello, Mr. Barraclough, I—"

He waved his helmet about.

"No, dun't tell me, dun't tell me . . . Are you a historic figure? I'm thinking the woolly tights. Your rain hat, the slight roll as you walk. Are you Nelson? I'm right, aren't I?"

I said, "I'm not doing mime. I'm just collecting—"

"Ah, the good days are back again. I've missed you. I really have. You and your friends, the STUDENTS. Monday, I will once more hear the sound of you cantering to Dither Hall on your imaginary ponies."

Actually, Vaisey did have an imaginary pony. Black Beauty.

Had he been spying on us?

Ruby came back and handed a letter to me.

She said, "Don't go daft."

I took the letter and said to her, "Heeee-heee, why should I go daft, it's only a letter from, you know, a mate to another mate, heeee, I don't know what you mean."

She just looked at me and shook her hair.

Then she said to her dad, "How did The Iron Pies rehearsal go?"

He said, "Bloody marvelous. The Iron Pies are going to be the biggest thing this side of Grimbottom. We are quite literally a sound sensation."

Ruby said, "Oh yeah? How many songs have you got?"

"Well, fust of all, we've done some belters for the mums and dads. All with the original pie theme."

Ruby said, "Like what?"

Mr. Barraclough said, "The well-known James Bond themes, 'For Your Pies Only,' 'Golden Pie,' and 'From Russia with a Pie.' Then a bit of a classic for the rockers, 'Rock Around the Pie.' And a few standard Beatles numbers, 'The Long and Winding Pie,' 'All You Need Is Pies,'

'Lucy in the Pie with Diamonds.' We'll be cracking. I'll have groupies trying to get hold of my pies."

I didn't know what to say, and I also didn't want to think about his pies anymore . . . I was dying to read my letter. So I said I had to go because Dibdobs was waiting for me.

I ran across the green and into Dandelion Cottage. Harold was back from his knitting workshop and I had to do more hugging duties with him. Then I started yawning to give him the idea of beddy-byes, but he said, "Tallulah, before you go up the wooden stairs to Noddsville, let me just show you my new cloak. It's hand-knitted, and as you can see it has shell buttons."

As he was swishing around modeling it for me, he said, "You see, the shells show man's connection with the earth or, in this case, Skegness beach."

At last I was in my squirrel room. I have my squirrel lamp switched on by my bed, and outside the wind is howling across the moors. But I am snug inside with my letter.

My letter from the Dream Boy.

I paused before I opened it.

To drink in its atmosphere of boyness.

Then I sniffed it.

And licked it.

I don't know why.

I'm turning into Matilda.

Ooooh. I can imagine him writing it. With a quill pen probably. A candle guttering late at night in his room. He is wearing his usual late-night wear—velveteen breeches and flouncy shirt. I don't know why his shirt is wet as he writes. Maybe he has been for a midnight swim. Or a late-night, fully clothed bath.

To cool his ardor and passions, which are running riot.

He looks out of his window over the moonlit dales, thinking of me as he last saw me in late summer. My long dark tresses framing my face. Looking up at him with my green eyes. And as he looks long and deep into my eyes, I feel an urge to raise my bottom eyelids and . . .

Hang on a minute—I have changed into an owlet!!!

Get a grip, Tallulah!!

I opened the envelope.

Here goes:

Dear Tallulah,

Hello, Green Eyes, welcome back to Heckmondwhite and the dizzy world of showbiz!

Well done for making it to the new term—personally, I think it was your spectacular Sugar Plum Bikey that did it. I don't think any of us who were there will forget your skirt catching in the back spokes, and you flying off into the backstage area.

Top.

I am off to Liverpool tonight to start my course but hope to see you in a couple of weeks when I come home. Good luck.

Knock 'em dead, but try not to break a leg! OR ANYONE ELSE'S.

Lots of love,

Alex

xxx

Mmmmmmmmmmmmmmm.

Outside in the dark I can hear an owl hooting. It will be big Connie out there, collecting food for the owlets.

She is holding her own mouse massacre. Ruby says the owlets will start hunting for themselves in a week or two. Having to do their own hunting will be a shock for them. They probably think there is a big owl in the sky that just hands them stuff.

I don't think you would poo in front of the big owl in the sky. At the same time as eating. Pooing and eating doesn't seem right to me.

Still, what does make sense in Nature?

Anyway to heck with Nature.

I'm not interested in Nature. I am only interested in Alex.

Alex in his velveteen breeches.

And flouncy shirt.

Alex who said, “Hello, Green Eyes.”

And, “Hope to see you in a couple of weeks.”

And who said, “Lots of love.”

And put three kisses.

That Alex.

I am keeping his letter under my pillow. Maybe I should write a letter back. Hmmm.

Night-night, Dream Boy.

Night-night, world.

I'm not an ice cream, I'm a human being!

THE NEXT DAY I woke up to the pitter-pattering of light hail on my window. The church bells chimed nine o'clock but it's still so dark it could be nighttime. I got out of my snuggly squirrel bed and had a look out of the window. Brrrr. This is the life, minus fifty degrees. There is a slight frost on the window. On the inside. When I rubbed it away I could see that even the sheep are huddling together for warmth.

And they are practically walking jumpers.

I don't know what to wear. Something cozy but glam. Thick tights and my new short green wool skirt, black top, and new leather over-the-knee boots?

And a hat so that the hail can't take all the bouncy bounce out of my hair.

I don't want the Tree Sisters to think I have let myself go.

When I was fully togged up, I went downstairs into the kitchen.

Even though it is Antarctic conditions, the Dobbinses have left a note to say that after church they are going out on their Earth Sky walk with the young Christian Table Tennis Team. They were sorry I was missing it. Well, they are on their own there!

I had a crumpet and some honey and milky coffee. The honey is local of course. Harold is obsessed with local produce. I bet he knows the bees by name. And has made them little winter cloaks like his. And is paying their tuition fees to Bee Academy. So they can better themselves and get out of the worker-bee trap.

Oooooh, I am so excited my legs are wiggling around for no reason. They are uncontrollable. They might calm down when I shove them in my boots.

I feel soooo lucky to be here. It feels great to have proper friends and to be on the brink of being a showbiz legend. Or, well, being on the course.

I know it's childish but I wanted to dance and sing with pleasure. I only wish I could do either.

Anything goes in the crazy world of theater, dahling. I might be discovered and asked to be Maria in *The Sound of Music* in the West End. That would make Alex know I was proper girlfriend material, and not some little girl with nobbly knees.

I can imagine myself in the Swiss Alps actually. In a big flouncy dress dancing with goats. "'The hills are alive with the sound of music . . . lalalala . . . with songs they have sung for a thousand years . . .'"

I got bundled up in my coat and hat and left the house. I had to walk slightly bent because there was a mini gale blasting across the moors and fields. But at least it had stopped hailing.

The sheep were still huddled together against the wind.

Looking at me.

I shouted to the sheep. "I love you, my little woolly friends."

They didn't like it. They didn't want to be my friends. They wanted to be my unfriends. They shuffled off as a group and tried to get in the hedge. And looked at me from there.

They are very cross-eyed.

Maybe it is so they can see round corners?

That would be handy if there were wolves creeping up behind you.

Hang on—your eyes should go outward to do that, not inward so that you just see your own looming nose. How useful would that be?

Anyway, I can't be bothered about the animal kingdom,

I am too busy being in a good mood. I'm going to do run-run-leap to *The Sound of Music* to keep me warm. Run, run, leap . . . "The hills are alive with the sound of . . ."

Oh great balls of fire. Leaning against the gate of the churchyard, like a great dark crow, was him. The Dark Force of Heckmondwhite. The Black Hearted Prince himself. Cain.

Cain Hinchcliff.

He was dressed all in black, a long black coat and black boots. He had his collar turned up against the wind. His hair is longer than when I last saw him. And it looks even blacker. He saw me, so I stopped leaping and started pretending that my boots were falling down. A half smile crossed his face. Not a nice beamy smile, a dark twisty smile. He pushed his hair back and looked me right in the eyes. His eyes are so black you can't tell what he is thinking. I know what I am thinking. I am thinking, Oh, banana skins and bejesus, he's seen me leaping, and talking to sheep.

Cain licked his lips like a hungry wolf and said, "Well, well, well . . . it's the young Southern lass back."

Then he ran his eyes up and down my body and said, "Tha's grown a bit."

Oh, how bloody well dare he?! How could he see through my coat? Maybe he had X-ray vision. What color pants had I got on? Oh, stop it, of course he couldn't see through my coat and see my pants. He was just being him. Rude and crude and horrible.

If I had my handbag I would hit him with it. I only had my hat or my mittens and that didn't seem nearly violent enough.

He was like an animal in trousers. Still, on the other hand, he had said I'd grown a bit, which means, I'd grown a bit. Not that I care what he thinks.

As the wind plucked at his hair and whipped it round his face, I remembered the last time I had seen him. It was in the barn and he was poking the owlets with a little stick.

All dark, with his dark broody eyes. And his black hair. And his long black eyelashes.

He's not good like Alex. Good and tall and brown-haired Alex. With his frilly shirt and his eyes and so on . . . he's . . .

He was still just staring at me.

He doesn't seem to know that staring is rude.

Well, two can play at that game.

I stared back.

And I'm not going to blink either. That will show him.

Then he stopped staring and came toward me and did up-close staring. His face was only about a foot away from mine.

Looking right in my eyes.

He said, "Tha's got eyes like a wild cat."

I could out-stare him any day.

Any day.

It suddenly started to hail quite heavily. I could hear

the pattering and bouncing on my hat. I could see the hailstones on his dark hair, hanging there like handfuls of pearls. He didn't seem to notice. Just went on staring right into my eyes. Then I felt a hailstone hit my face. It didn't just ping off—it started slipping slowly down the middle of my forehead. Then it got to my eyebrows and I thought it had gone. But then I felt it start slipping down the side of my nose, like a tear. I went on staring. He was not going to win this staring competition. I could feel the hailstone had just got to my nostril when . . . still staring at me . . .

He did this thing.

He stepped right up to me, so I nearly went cross-eyed trying to keep staring and . . . then he licked his lips and put his tongue out and . . . and . . .

And he LICKED off the hailstone.

He was licking my nose. I could feel his hot, soft tongue on my nose.

And he was staring at me while he did it.

What? *What?!*

This wasn't right.

This wasn't even on Cousin Georgia's snogging scale.

This was just wrong.

Very, very wrong.

Then a girl's voice behind him shouted, "Oy, Cain. What's tha doing? I've been waiting by the bike shed like tha said for half a bloody hour."

He was licking my face!

Like I was an ice cream!

I nearly said, "I am not an ice cream! I am a human being!"

He said softly to me, "Tasty."

Then he took a step back and turned around slowly. Behind him I saw Beverley approaching. Cain turned back to me and smiled his mean smile. Then he smiled his mean smile and made a clicking noise like you do when you say giddyup to a horsie. As he swished his coat round and walked off up the hill toward the moors I could see that Beverley didn't look pleased to see me.

She didn't say, "Gosh, how nice to see you again, Tallulah, on this inclement morning." Had she seen the licking incident? She just stood with her arms folded looking at me. Even though it was hailing, she only had on a short-sleeved jumper.

She had very big arms. Very big. Her dad had a potato farm so she probably did quite a bit of heavy lifting. Maybe if I said something nice to her, you know, like, "Ooooh, your arms are a . . . good . . . shape," she might not hurt me.

Cain kept on walking up the hill while she stood there looking at me.

Cain called back, "Beverley, is tha coming wi' me or are tha going to stand there gabbing all day?"

Beverley went after him but turned back and said in a loud, mean voice, "You and your posh stuckup mates keep your hands off our lads . . . or else. Think on."

I was thinking of something to say when Cain whistled and his big black dog came bounding over the hedge with a rabbit in its mouth. Every time I saw Cain something died. Cain gave the dog a brief pat on its head and said, "Good Dog. You've got our supper then."

Beverley caught up to him. She said to Cain, "You treat that dog better'n tha treats me."

Cain said, "Beverley, the dog can fetch sticks, it can catch rabbits . . . it dun't moan on. Can you do that? No."

He was unbelievable.

I was so shocked at the nose-licking incident I was unable to move. As they disappeared off over the brow of the hill, Rubster came running along, her pigtails going berserk. Matilda was running alongside her and tried to stop when she saw me, but the momentum of her tummy made her go past me and collide with the hedge.

Ruby panted, "Were that Cain with Beverley? Uh-oh, he likes trouble that lad, Beverley's mum will be on the warpath big-time if she finds out."

I didn't say anything to Ruby. What was there to say? "Cain has just licked my face?" I must never think of it again. I must put it out of my mind and think only of my letter from Alex. Alex the Good, who would never lick a girl's face.

We got to the bus stop just as it came careering round the corner. Hurrah!!!! I was so excited about seeing my chums. The bus juddered to a stop and the door opened and . . . Jo jumped off! All little and dark and excited. With her dark eyes gleaming. Like a human conker, but with legs and arms. And a head. She hadn't changed. Still as mad as a hen. A violent hen. She ran and punched Ruby's arm, and then mine, and then both at the same time. She was yelling, "TALLULAH! THE RUBSTER!"

Vaisey was smoothing her red curls as she came down the steps. She looked at me as she got her rucksack down and smiled a little shy smile. Oh, I had missed that turny-up nose and freckles and that roundy waggly bottom (and the other bits in between). I ran over and hugged her to me, and then she hugged me and Ruby, going "Oh, Lullah, Lullah and little Ruby!!"

And a tear came out of the corner of her eye. She was saying, "Oh, oh, oh," and jumping up in little jumps as we hugged. Jo was running round and round us in circles and Matilda was following her.

Flossie was last off. Blimey, I think she might have grown. Her fringe has. It is down to the middle of her glasses so that you can't see if she's got a forehead.

She gathered us all in a big bear hug. The comrades together again. A feast of talent! Our tights runneth over.

Flossie said, in a deep Texan accent, which is weird as she's from Blackpool, "Why, y'all, here we damned are—the Tree Sisters and li'l old Ruby Mae, back again at the old corral!!! This calls for a damn special celebration dance, let's show these here people our rootin' tootin' dance. Come on, Lullah Mae, we'll do the tune. And you dance."

So I did it.

I did the thing that I can do.

My special talent.

I did my spontaneous Irish dancing.

And as I flung my legs around with gay abandon my thespian chums sang, "Hiddly diddly diddly diddle."

That well-known Irish song that no one has ever heard of because it doesn't exist.

Happy days.

I felt once more the golden slippers of applause.

Cain Hinchcliff will not be spoiling my life.

In fact, I will never be thinking about him again.

With his nose-licking ways.

Why would he do that? Why.

Bob the technician from Dother Hall was coming to pick the girls up later in his Bobmobile, so we had time to swap news before he arrived. We went and sat on the wall next to The Blind Pig while Rubes went to get some nourishing, warming winter snacks. It's handy having a little pub friend.

Oooh, it's good to be back. It had stopped hailing and we snuggled into our coats for a goss.

Vaisey is looking forward to seeing Jack again, her maybe boyfriend.

She said, "He gave me his plectrum to remind me of him."

I put my arm around her and said, "That's plucky of him."

And they all laughed. Which is nice. I felt all warmy. Even my knees. Rubes came back with the nourishing winter snacks—cheese and onion crisps, salt and vinegar crisps, two pickled eggs, and some pork scratchings. It was like being in heaven.

Flossie said, "This is my plan for the term—I am going to become a superstar and have three or four boyfriends. I've grown my fringe especially."

Jo was chomping through two packets of crisps at the same time but managed to say, "I've had loads of letters and phone calls from Phil!! Loads. Every day."

I said, "Woo-hoo! So is he like your official boyfriend?"

Jo went a bit red and said, "Well, he told me about his campaign to let people know that he's not all bad and that he has a serious side."

We looked at her.

I said, "But he doesn't have a serious side."

Jo got a bit defensive. "He has, actually, he's joining in with the police to help them . . . with the out-of-control yoof."

I said, "He IS the out-of-control yoof."

Vaisey said, "Help the police? What, like an informer?"

Flossie said, "Is he called 'Phil-the-policeman's-friend' now?"

Jo went red. "No, it's a campaign. It's to let the police know that teenage boys are people too."

I said, "But that's a lie, isn't it? My brother isn't a person."

Flossie said, "I'm not being rude or anything, but what could Phil help the police with?"

Jo said, "Phil's good at loads of things."

We looked at her.

Jo said, going even redder, "Well, he's really excellent at . . . erm . . . kissing."

I said, "That's not what policemen like, is it though? They don't like being kissed by teenage boys."

Vaisey said, "Policemen don't like being kissed by babies but Phil, er, he's quite, well, he's not a baby, is he?"

Flossie said, "If he's going around kissing policemen, he's a dead man."

As we chomped away, thinking about kissing policemen, three very big girls I had never seen before came lumbering up. They looked at us like we were snot girls, then they sat on the wall at the other side of the Blind Pig courtyard and started chewing gum.

Ruby said quietly, "Oh, bloody hell, it's the other Bottomly sisters, Chastity, Diligence, and Ecclesiastica."

I started to laugh.

"Ecclesiastica? Does she get called Eccles for short?"

Ruby said, "No. Dun't start, they're Bible names and they don't think it's funny. The Bottomlys dun't think owt is funny, except fighting. In between bus driving, their mam does cage fighting in Leeds."

Chas, Dil, and Eccles, as I called them (quietly in my brain), were looking at us and then they lit up fags.

I whispered out of the corner of my mouth, "Are they going to get their pipes out next?"

One of them shouted across, "What are you stuckup madams looking at?"

Oh dear.

Ruby said, "That's Ecclesiastica. You're lucky she's in a good mood."

Mr. Barraclough came out of The Blind Pig and said to Ruby, "Rubes, say night-night to the thespians, it's school tomorrow."

The Bottomly sisters started laughing and going, "Oooooohhh, it's SCHOOL t'morra. Say night-night."

Mr. Barraclough glanced at the Bottomly sisters and said, "Hello, ladies." Then he turned to go off into the pub.

Ecclesiastica drew on her fag and said, "Ay up, Grandad."

Ruby sat down and said, "Oh, well, that's done it."

There was a bit of a quiet moment, then Mr. Barraclough turned around and said to Ecclesiastica, "Is my wall comfortable enough for your enormous arse, dear? Or is it time you took it somewhere else?" And the other two sisters sniggered. Eccles went a sort of dull red color but she didn't move—she just kept looking at Mr. Barraclough.

He said, "Well, I've tried to be nice, but I can see I will have to go the whole hog."

Ruby said, "Dad. Not the . . ."

He looked at her sorrowfully. "I'm as sorry as you are, Ruby, but it has to be done."

Ted went into the pub and came back a moment later with his Viking helmet on and a photograph. He came and showed it to us. It was the picture of him with a gun standing on a pile of pies. Underneath it said, *Ted Barraclough, champion pie eater. 22 steak and kidney, 4 pork.*

Then he walked across and showed it to the Bottomly sisters, and said to them, "Have some respect, girls. Thy father only ate ten pies and then had to go and have a bit of a lie down, so bog off somewhere else."

The Bottomly sisters looked at him and then they got up and sloped off.

Ted went back into the pub singing, "I am the king of hellfire!!! PIES, I'm gonna teach you to burn. PIES, I'm gonna teach you to learn!!"

I went to bed happy after seeing the Tree Sisters. But I gave my nose a good scrub in case any of Cain's molecules had got into it. And besides, I am sleeping on Alex's letter and don't want to besmirch it.

There's no people like show people

I WOKE UP EARLY the next day partly because I'm excited about starting college but also because it was like sleeping in a zoo.

Birds had been tweeting and carrying on in the trees outside my window practically since I'd gone to bed. How can anyone sleep in the country? I think some of the birds have got secret mouth organs. And drums. Like a really bad band rehearsing. A band of birds singing with no tune. Like those people in bygone days who wore black polo-necks and played jazz that had no tune. Beatniks they were called. I think my dad was one. Hey, perhaps the birds are . . . beakniks!!!

Not beatniks but BEAK-niks.

I must write that down in my notebook because one

day it may be comedy gold.

Especially if I do a bird opera.

Which I might. Following on from the triumph of my bicycle ballet.

I could call it *Feather*!

Or maybe *Saturday Night Feather*!

We Will Flock You!

Grouse!

Pheasant of the Opera.

Right, so this is the official start to my performing-arts notebook.

I need a name for my secret notebook.

What shall I call it?

What does the book suggest? I looked at the cover. Plums, dark . . .

Dark, fruit . . . unanswered questions . . . questions that need answering.

Something like . . .

The Darkly Demanding Damson Diary.

That's me, that is.

It's going to be my spontaneous stream of consciousness. Here goes . . .

I'll start a new page after the Labradad entry. I may need to add drawings, and so on, of the Labradad. So I'll start a new blank page and begin. Right, I'm just going to go mad and improvise. I'm going to let myself go and not censor myself at all. Let my pen flow over the pages.

Oh, hang on, I'll just get a pen that has a thicker point.

Hmmmm, good, good. Nice thick pen. Right.

Now, my stream of consciousness begins . . . No, no, my feet are all wrong. No one can improvise with squirrel slippers on. I'll put my ballet shoes on for inspiration. Yes, good, good. Ballet shoes, good. And . . . oh, crikey, now I've got the squirrel slipper's tail sticking in my bottom . . . I'll just . . . anyway, off we jolly well go . . .

Aaaah, once again I can smell the crowd and hear the roar of the greasepaint. This is where I belong. I want to go to the tippy top of the toppermost. I know that Sidone Beaver has said that we will pay the price of fame.

She said, "Your feet will bleed before you wear the golden slippers of applause."

I am ready. I am girding my feet and my loins to suffer what I have to for my art. Here in the wilds of Yorkshire I feel the spirit of Charlotte Brontë filling my snug winter tights. And in my heart I hold the letter from Alex. And so my Winter of Love begins with his letter.

Performance note:

When I say I am holding the letter from Alex with my heart, I don't mean this in a weird way.

I know that hearts can't hold letters really.

Although I could make a papier-mâché heart with little arms.

I hid the diary under my pillow with Alex's letter in the back of it. I will start my letter to him tonight.

When I went down the wooden stairs to the kitchen, Dobbins was trying to dress the lunatic twins for school. Max looked at me and smiled his sock animal smile.

He looks even more not normal.

Oh, I see. He's got goggles on. And a swimming hat. Cripes, it's scary. Goggle Boy came for his morning knee hug.

"Ug oo, Lullah. I's a wimmen."

What? He's a woman now? Overnight?

I managed to escape with minimal hugging. Dibdobs was red-faced and breathless.

"Hello, Tallulah dear, there's a boiley egg for you, but I . . . Will you take the goggles off, Sam dear, I can't get your beret on."

Sam biffed her with his snorkel and knocked her glasses sideways.

"NO, LADY. I's a WIMMEN too!!!!!"

Dibdobs was trying to put a beret over the top of his swimming hat.

You can't say she doesn't try.

Dibdobs said, "It's not swimming till this afternoon."

Max said, "Shhhh, lady."

They were wearing snorkels and berets when they left. They'll never make any normal friends.

Five minutes later, I was staggering through the village to the path that leads to Dother Hall. For once it isn't snowing or raining but there is a gale force wind blowing. Ruby yelled across at me from The Blind Pig, "Ay, come and say good-bye to Matilda, she wants to show you summat."

When I struggled over to the shelter of Ruby's front door, Matilda went dogtastic.

Leaping up at me.

She has her ballet tutu on! It really suits her. And I notice she is wearing a little satchel on top of it.

Ruby said, "She's got her playtime snacks in it."

I said to Matilda, "Have you got your doggie treats in there? Have you got your ickle doggie bickies in there, have you?" She nuzzled me with her snout. Aaaah. I don't normally like animals nuzzling me, but she is so cute.

Then Ruby said, "Yep, she's got her snack hoofs."

"Hoofs?"

Ruby was going off down the path toward Blubberhouse. "Dad gets them from the farm when they slaughter a cow. He has the cow heels and Matilda has the cow hoofs."

This is not the kind of talk that a creative artiste listens to.

Especially one who has had her face licked by a hoof eater (Matilda).

And an animal in trousers (Cain).

Two face-lickings in as many days.

I was halfway to college in about ten minutes because the wind was behind me. As I passed by the sign that read *Woolfe Academy for Boys* (at about twenty miles an hour), I couldn't help thinking about Charlie again.

What was it going to be like when we bumped into each other?

I wish I could say he was a rubbish kisser.

Like bat boy.

But he wasn't. It was softy and made my legs feel a bit droopy and . . . it was the best kiss I've ever had. Well, in fact, it was the second kiss I've ever had. For all I know it might have been a Number 4 on Georgia's snogging scale, "a kiss lasting over three minutes without a break." I will never know though, because I didn't have a watch.

Anyway, I'm not going to ever think about it again. About how he kissed me, and then said this is wrong, I've got a girlfriend.

And another thing, has nose-licking even happened to anyone else? There is no mention of it in *Jane Eyre*, is there? Even when Mr. Rochester is blinded, he doesn't go for Jane's nose.

I might have to write to Cousin Georgia, like an agony

snogging aunt, and ask her advice about nose-licking.

I still can't believe he did that.

Cain Hinchcliff.

Perhaps he's one of Fang's adopted children. Only he's half-dog, half–complete moron. Only.

There is a poster on the village hall to say that his band, The Jones, is playing on Saturday night.

Ruby said that she doesn't think they will play, though, because of the big fight they had when Cain got off with Ruben's girlfriend. She thinks they have split up again.

They are like wild animals. The whole family, Seth, Ruben, Cain. They are all bad.

Not good.

Not like Alex. He wouldn't lick someone's nose.

Or destroy an outdoor lavatory.

He's not a nose-licking, lavatory-destroying sort of guy.

He is a dreamy sort of guy.

And good.

Then I rounded the corner and there it was, just as I remembered, Dother Hall. The rambling manor house with its turrets and its mullioned windows. Its magnificent Gothic chimneys towering into the wind-tossed sky. Blaise Fox took me up there and told me I could be Heathcliff. She said I had a "special quality" and . . .

Hang on a minute!

A spooky figure was staggering about up there on the roof. Dancing? A mad person dancing on the roof. Like a scene from *Jane Eyre*. Could it be the ghost of mad Mrs. Rochester?

I had a strange sense of déjà vu.

As I got closer, I could see that it wasn't Mrs. Rochester. It was Bob the technician.

Up on the roof. Like he was the first time I turned up at Dother Hall.

In fact it wasn't déjà vu.

It was déjà Bob.

What was going on? He seemed to be fighting a black parachute. On the roof. I don't think gale force conditions are a time to go parachuting.

I pushed the heavy front door open and went into the front hall, which was a tumbling mass of hysterical girls. The noise level was a million decibels. Gudrun Sachs, Sidone's assistant, looked even madder than I remember. She was in dungarees and had her clipboard out. She was shouting, "Girls, girls, calm down, let's have some quiet while I take the register."

No one took any notice. Everyone was too busy screeching, although some girls were practicing ballet positions. Or a bit of tap.

In the end Gudrun blew a whistle and shouted, "*Achtung!!!!*"

I was looking for the Tree Sisters when I heard a really

posh voice behind me say, "Railly, railly nice to see you again."

There they were—Lavinia, Anoushka, and Davinia. Lav, Noos, and Dav. The girls from the year above.

Lav was smiling at me. She looks even slimmer than she did last term and her hair's all sleek and coppery. Even though she has a skirt and top on like mine, hers look about a million times more expensive. She said in a really bad Irish accent, "Bejesus, Tallulah, did you have a nice time in the old country, in Oireland, begorrah, begosh, bejesus?"

And she ruffled my hair.

Oh God.

I forced myself to smile and said, "Oh yes, well, hello."

Gudrun started waving at us like a maniac and yelling, "Come and get registered, girls. *Schnell, schnell!!*"

Lavinia snaked her arm around my shoulder like I was her bestie, and said to me, "I railly, railly want to see more of your performances this term, Lulles."

Lulles? Maybe I should call her "Lavs" as my own little joke. Yeah, I could say, "I'm just going round to the Lavs," and so on, hahahaha . . . oh, she is still going on.

"I know you had like a railly hard time last term, you know with your Sugar Plum Bikey." She looked at me and smiled a sympathetic smile. Which somehow made me want to poke my finger up her nose.

But she was STILL banging on.

"So I am railly determined to help you through this term. We could get together and try some ideas out."

Oh no.

She was still talking.

"Hey, Lulles, begorrah, bejesus, I have just had an IDEA. Doh, how stupid am I? Why didn't I think of it before? We could get our friend, you know, the boy from the pub, the one who has gone to Liverpool . . . Alex, that's it, isn't it? Yah, we could get him to come in and give us his professional opinion."

I said, "Oh yes, that is a great idea."

Oh yes, get Alex to come in so you can fawn all over my Alex.

My good Alex.

My Alex, who gives me three kisses on his letter.

Yes, I will let you fawn over him just as soon as I hear that hell is freezing over and has opened up a skating rink for fools.

I didn't actually say that, I said, "Hmmmmm mmm-mmm."

Anyway, he wrote a letter to me, not her, and when I write back, I will not mention her.

Then the assembly bell rang and Lav, Dav, and Noos went off into the main hall.

Flossie came over and put her arm around me and said, "What does she want? Does she love you?"

I said, "She ruffled my hair and she talked about eggs."

* * *

We finally got into the main hall—nothing seemed to have changed. The stage still has papier-mâché boulders on it from our end-of-term *Wuthering Heights.*

I based my Heathcliff on Cain Hinchcliff. Not the Irish dancing, that was just something my legs did all by themselves, but the shouting and stroppy badness. And the moaning was based on him. No licking though. Because I didn't know about it at the time.

It was quite gloomy in the hall because not many of the lights seemed to be working.

Flossie said, "Brr, it's cold in here. I got rained on in the dorm last night."

Jo said, "Wait till it snows, they will have to chip us out of our sheets. This place is falling down."

Vaisey was bobbling around, all excited. "Oh, Lullah, wasn't it good when you were Heathcliff and you came back from London all moody and mean and then you called for your dog, and Matilda came on in shades and a leather jacket!!!"

Vaisey was right, I was spiffing.

We linked up and looked about. There were loads of familiar faces, Milly and Tilly, Pippy and Becka. I couldn't believe my luck really. Here I was at a proper performing arts college. Away from home. Boys around! My own little gang.

I was so overcome with happiness that I gave a

spontaneous girl hug to Vaisey and said, "Pass it on." And she passed it on to Jo, and Flossie, and they passed it back. We started swaying and singing, "There's no people like show people!! They smile when they are down!"

I had my arm around Flossie and she was back in Texas in her head and she yelled, "Why, Miss Tallulah, take your goddam hand off my corker, I'm not that sort of laydee."

I shouted above the hubbub, "You know you love it, you lezzie."

I thought I would just try out some new words from my cousin Georgia. I'm not completely sure what they mean but . . . hey, I'm improvising!!!

At which point I felt a looming presence. Something behind me. A cold chill went through my body as I heard that dreaded familiar voice.

"So, Talluuuuulah Casey, regrettably we meet again. Remember I am watching you. I have my eyes on you. Always. Sit down."

I looked up into the stern, forbidding, beak-like face of Dr. Lightowler. We all sat down.

As she walked past us and up toward the front of the hall, Jo said softly, "She still hates you times-a-million."

Vaisey said, "She just loomed up from nowhere. Did she frighten you? She frightens me."

Flossie said, "Her beaky eyes are watching you wherever you go, even on the lavatory."

I said, "I think she is part owl because her hearing is—"

Blimey, she *is* part owl because as I spoke her head turned back toward me, but her body didn't! Just her head. Spooky dooky.

She looked at me, not blinking.

I looked back at her, not blinking. I couldn't help it.

We were two owls looking at each other.

I felt a little twitch in my lower lids.

A voice inside my head warned me, "No! Don't start raising your lower eyelids like your owl impression. It's not funny. It isn't funny."

Then another voice in my head said, "It IS funny. Go on, do it. It is very, very funny."

The first voice said, "Just do one eyelid, just a little eyelid raise. Or a slow blink. She'll never notice that."

Then my legs began to feel tingly and restless.

No, heavens, no! Not an owl impression and Irish dancing at the same time. She'll eat me alive!!!! Bit by bit . . . head first . . .

Save me!

But then thankfully she walked on. (Not with her head facing backward.)

As we sat there waiting for Sidone to arrive, Jo said, "Did you get a postcard from Honey?"

We all nodded.

Vaisey said, "I wonder what her big news is?"

I said, "She's probably done multiple snogging."

Vaisey said, "Multiple? Is that . . ." Then Monty came

onto the stage. Good Lord, he's wearing a pink leotard. Just. He is quite porky. He looks like he has got little snacks in his cheeks that he is saving for later.

Flossie said, "He's goddam beautiful."

But I don't think she really means it. Anyway, we gave Monty a big round of applause.

Monty was delighted to be back. His little piggy eyes were sparkly with enthusiasm for the theater.

He clapped his pudgy hands together. And gave us a little twirl.

"Mes enfants, mes enfants . . . l'aventure commence. The ADVENTURE commences. *Tout de suite. Immédiatement.* Once again, we at Dother Hall embark on the noblest of voyages, we are voyaging to the land of entertainment. Of magic!!! Of transformation."

And he did a spontaneous pas de deux.

Jo said, "If he does that again he won't be in that leotard for long."

I said, "No, he'll be in an ambulance."

Flossie punched my arm. And said in her Texan drawl, "Why, Miss Lullah, that was very nearly a goddam joke y'all told there."

Monty was still talking.

"And guiding us as always on our journey is our captain. Or should I say, our captain-ess! The brightest star in our firmament. The wick of our candles. The bow to our arrows. The beaver in our midst. Ms. Sidone Beaver!!!"

Monty skipped back and stood in third position as Sidone slowly came onto the stage.

She was wearing a riding outfit and a black, feathered hat. With an eye patch. And a riding whip.

Vaisey whispered to me, "That's what I wear when I am Black Beauty."

I whispered back, "What, you wear an imaginary eye patch when you are your imaginary horse?"

She said, "Yes."

I smiled to myself. This is the life. Proper friends who share everything together.

Sidone was looking at us. Her eye roving over the rows of expectant faces before her.

At last she spoke.

"My girls, my girls, once again we enter the theater of dreams. Our hearts filled with hope, our feet ready to bleed if necessary. Once more we strive, strive to reach the stars. Because, as the old saying, goes . . ."

Sidone was using her projecting voice. Rolling her "r"s and pausing a lot. Flicking her whip.

"All of us are lying in the gutter . . . but . . . some of us . . . are looking up at the stars!"

There was a round of applause and Monty pirouetted.

Sidone hadn't finished though. Her voice got very deep and emotional.

"And some of us are being spat upon by the taxman. But let me tell you, my girls, we shall not be spat upon and take it lying down. We shall rise up and wipe off the spit and turn it into clouds of stardust."

She swept off the stage and we all looked at each other. What did that mean?

Flossie said, "It doesn't say anything in my timetable about spitting."

Vaisey said, "I think she means it sort of metaphorically. You know, like pretend . . . spitting . . ."

Jo said, "So does that mean we're doing mime spitting?"

This is what performing arts is like. People, or "artists" as I suppose we are technically called, talking about mime spitting. It's the *thea-tah, dahlings*!!!!

After assembly, we drifted off to first lesson and I said to the others, "My cousin told me how to make boys like you. You go like this, flicky hair, flicky hair."

And I did flicky hair, flicky hair.

Then we all tried flicky hair, flicky hair as we walked along the corridor.

A voice behind me said, "Tallulah Casey, walk properly."

I looked after Dr. Lightowler as she swept down the corridor, her cloak billowing behind her.

I said, "Why me? Why does she hate me? Maybe she holds my knees against me."

We had Monty first thing. He had managed to get out of his leotard and had his tweedy suit on and a waistcoat.

He clapped his pudgy hands together and said, "Oh, girls, joy of joys, once more we go back to the Bard. William, William, William Shakespeare. As you know, our group project this term is *A Midsummer Night's Dream*, his hilarious romantic comedy. Ah, the puzzle that is romance!! *Le grand amour.* The dreams, the fantasies. I remember in Copenhagen a dark night, the stars peeping from the firmament, probably looking down in amusement at the antics of us humans wandering around the Reeperbahn. Giggling, dancing, high on the emotions of *la romance.* I said to Biffo . . . well, well, never mind. What larks, girls! What larks!"

Vaisey and a few of the girls have been in productions of *A Midsummer Night's Dream* before. But I had never even read it. After hearing about Monty and Biffo in the Reeperbahn I am not sure I want to.

Monty said, "But I will show you what I am going to do with the sacred text. I'm going to do this."

And he kissed his copy of *A Midsummer Night's Dream* and then flung it to the floor dramatically.

He looked at us.

"You are thinking I have gone mad. How can I throw the Bard to the floor? And indeed I can't."

He picked up the book. "But what I am saying, girls, is that William would want us to make our own connection with the feelings of love and dreams and with his poetry. You have a young person's idea of love, you must explore this for yourselves . . . not be led by someone like me who 'hath the gray bearde.'"

Jo said, "Erm, who hath the gray bearde?"

I whispered behind my book. "Monty certainly hasn't. He hasn't even got the gray mustachey."

Monty the Beardless was still talking and musing. "Of course, read, read, read the original, girls, his text, drink in the words of his genius. Immerse yourself in the poetry of confused love and imaginary asses."

Flossie snorted. Monty didn't notice.

"But in true Dother Hall style, we are going to give the play a modern spin. Go a little bit . . . avant garde!!! Just to give you an idea and a flavor, I have taken one of the fairy verses and turned it into a song."

He got out a tambourine and started singing, "I am that merry wanderer of the night . . ."

And started tap-dancing.

At break I saw Dav and Lav looking over at us.

Lav waved at me. She called over, "We'll show them what we Oirish can do, bejesus."

Vaisey said, "She's really taken to you, hasn't she? Is it because she's Irish as well?"

I said, "No, but her dad has got an Irish gardener."

Please don't let her be my new best friend.

I said to Vaisey, "I hope she doesn't try to be my mental."

She said, "Mentor."

I said, "I know what I mean."

Flossie said, "I'm going to ask Honey how she manages having a few boyfwends on the go. Because if I got the knack I could have Seth and maybe even that nice Charlie as a sort of side dish and that still leaves room for meeting someone at The Jones's gig on Saturday."

What?? Why was she talking about Charlie? Not that I care as I am forgetting about him. Whoever he is.

Flossie said, "Actually, speaking about Charlie, I thought he quite liked you, Lullah. It's funny that he didn't ask you to the cinema last term. I thought he was going to, didn't you?"

Vaisey said, "Yeah, so did I!"

I said, "Mmmmmmmffff."

Which just about sums it up, actually.

We didn't get the chance to say anything else because the bell rang and we had Monty. Again. For French.

Not that it makes much difference what we have Monty for. It always ends up being about him and Biffo and Sprogsy at drama college.

French was mostly listening to Monty tell us about his youth in *le* gay *Paree*. And guess who was there?

"*Mais oui*, we had such a gay camaraderie, Biffo and Sprogsy and I." He started chuckling fatly. "Let me illustrate, with the aid of my training in clowning, a *très amusant* incident that happened." He put on a big red nose and started acting out the surprise he got when Biffo and Sprogsy pushed him into the Seine.

As he splashed about on the floor shouting, *"Au secours . . . vous êtes méchant!!"* we started passing notes to each other.

Flossie wrote:

Bonjour Mon Arbre Sisters,
I 'ave ze plan. Zis is mon three or four boyfriend plan. Je commence on Saturday at le gig. I am going to make Seth Hinchcliff my plaything.
Au revoir

How can she even think about having anything to do with that family?

At lunch we got togged up in our hats and coats and slouched out through the gates. It was freezing. We linked arms for warmlies as we crunched over the dead leaves and fallen-down branches. The woods have changed since we were last here. Not many leaves on any of the trees.

Suddenly I felt all wistful and autumny and said sadly, "The woods have gone all baldy."

Jo was scampering ahead. "Baldy-smaldy, it's just trees. I wonder if the lads will be out and about. Do you think so, do you? I know they are back today because Phil told me it was the same day as us."

Vaisey said, "It would be really nice to see Jack but maybe it's a bit too soon. I mean, it's only the first day . . . and anyway, does my hair look a bit, a bit . . ."

I said, "Mad?"

As Vaisey started smoothing down her curls she looked at my head. "Lullah, you've got a bit of twig in your hair. Shall I pick it out?"

I let her pick the twig out of my hair not because I wanted to impress the boys. It was just too twiggy.

I said to Jo, "Did Phil say he would meet you today at the tree? At lunchtime?"

Flossie said, "Did you tell him to bring some mates for me? Like a mate should."

Jo started spontaneously smashing up a big mound of toadstools with a stick. She said, "If someone has been talking to you every day and then didn't get in touch for two whole days is there a secret boy meaning in that?"

I don't know.

I said, "My cousin Georgia says that boys are like gazelles. She says they get alarmed when they get close to girls. And have to leap off to the woods like gazelles in trousers. Or have I just made that up?"

Vaisey said, "Gazelles in trousers? But gazelles have got four legs, haven't they? So that's two pairs of trousers really . . ."

Jo put her hand over Vaisey's mouth.

Flossie said, "Well, what did Phil say when he last spoke to you?"

Jo said, "He said, 'See you later.'"

Uh-oh. What did that mean? When was later? Was later today? Or was that too early for later?

I found myself rambling out loud.

"I didn't know that being a girl was such hard work. Did you? I sort of thought you went along looking like a boy for a bit then your corkers started growing, and that was it. I tried to ask Mum once about girl stuff. And she said, 'Just be yourself' and went off to the Netherlands to paint bikes."

Vaisey said, "I know. I didn't know whether to bring my plectrum or not. And anyway what does giving someone a plectrum mean? It might not mean what a girl thinks it means. It might not be nice. A boy might mean, here's a plectrum, now go and get your *own* guitar and play it. It would be good if Honey was here because she knows a lot."

Jo said, "But we didn't have a row or anything, I didn't do any more shouting than normal. Why would he just not phone me?"

I said bitterly, "I don't know. Why do boys be nice to you and then, er, not be?"

Vaisey said cheerfully, "Maybe Phil, well, he's quite physical, isn't he? Maybe he broke his hand when he was helping the police . . . and couldn't write or phone with it."

Flossie looked at her. "He would have to have broken both hands, wouldn't he?"

Vaisey shook her curls. "Yes, that will be it, he kept on helping the police after he'd broken one hand and then the other one . . . broke."

Flossie said, "That's a bit unrealistic, Vaisey. Maybe, maybe he got sudden eczema of the head and was . . ."

I said, "Too shy to say?"

Flossie nodded.

I said, "Or, it may have been . . . boils. Adolescent boils."

I have just realized I've still got my dance tights on. They don't exactly hide my knees. And what would I do if Charlie was there? Should I ignore him? Perhaps he would ignore me? I must ignore him first. Just in case.

I'm a nervous wreck now.

When we got to our special tree it was all quiet. And a bit eerie. The forest was very still and there was no scuttling or snuffling going on. It was too damp to sit down so we had to eat our lunch standing up.

In between munching, I said, "Apparently if you want to get a boy to like you, you go sort of mysterious and icy and cool. That's what my cousin said and she has loads of boyfriends and snogging-type experiences."

Vaisey said, "So how do you do that? Be mysterious and icy and cool? Like a human icicle? Because I could try it out on Jack. If I ever see him again. Maybe Cain has told him not to see me after the last time, you know, with a gig coming up and everything."

I said, "Well, I don't want to be the fly in the dancing tights, but nothing would surprise me about Cain Hinchcliff after what he did."

Vaisey was still keen on the icicle idea. "How do you do the icicle thing, Lullah?"

I said without really thinking it through, "Well, I did sort of try the icicle thing on Cain Hinchcliff, but he's not really a boy, he's an animal in trousers."

Flossie said, "Yum yum, an animal in trousers. They're handsome, though, the Hinchcliffs—mean, moody, and magnificent. Yum yum, animals in trousers."

We all looked at her.

"Well, you said Cain was like an animal in trousers. Seth's his brother so he must be an animal in trousers as well. Goodie."

I said, "Er, I didn't mean that being an animal in trousers was a good thing . . . and also they have destroyed a lavatory."

Flossie was floating about in the deep dark South in her mind. She did her drawl.

"Now, I know that Seth he dun no good. He's no good, y'all, and I kinda know he done wrong, but I can't help myself, he's got animal magnetism."

I said, "Well, it's probably the ferrets he keeps down his trousers."

Jo wasn't interested in ferrets. She said, "So what happened when you tried this icicle thing on Cain?"

Damn.

They were all looking at me, so I finished my tuna surprise and I improvised. I had to share the hailstone thing with the Tree Sisters.

"Well, I will tell you how it happened. It was like this. The day you all arrived on the bus from Skipley, I was on my way to meet you. An icy, cruel wind was blowing in from Grimbottom. Savage and cold, the kind that freezes socks and underpants on lines. Wild creatures scuttled to their dark lairs; sheep stood cross-eyed in hedges, looking at their noses. And that was when I saw him. Him. As it began to hail, he was standing by the fence like a heathen rusty crow."

Hmmm, I must remember to put this in my performance notebook. *A heathen rusty crow.*

Vaisey spoiled it of course. I think she must have been an egghead, or an elephant, in a previous life.

She said, "A rusty crow? Do you mean, that he was like a metal crow that had been out in the rain and . . ."

Jo said, "Yeah, what's a 'heathen' crow? Is that a crow that doesn't go to church?"

I went on, before they all got into the crow business.

"When he saw me, he said in his cruel broad accent, 'So, it's the soft Southern lass back again.' He was taunting me like he always did. But this time was different. I had changed. I had grown."

Flossie said, "Are you talking corker-wise?"

I ignored her and trod on her foot as I continued.

"I looked into his black, tainted eyes and felt courage stir in my breast."

Flossie said, "Good, good. I'm a bit worried about the one breast though. Shouldn't you say, 'stirred in my breasts'?"

"No."

Flossie was still thinking about the breasts. "Or what about 'stirred in my corker area'? Or 'even my corkers stirred'?"

I went on. "I said to him, 'Cain Hinchcliff. I hate you. I hate you from the depths of my soul.'"

Jo punched my arm. "Well done, girl."

Flossie looked at me. Through her glasses from underneath her fringe.

I said, "What?"

She just kept looking.

I said, "What are you doing looking? Is that all you can do? Look and look?"

She was still looking.

I said, "All right, I didn't quite say that."

She said, "What did you say?"

I looked down at the ground and mumbled.

"I didn't get a chance to say anything. He licked a

hailstone off my face and went off."

Now all of them looked at me.

Flossie said, "Cain licked your face? He LICKED your face . . . he licked your FACE?"

I've got my new timetable. There's all sorts on it that I have no idea about. What is "Theater of the Absurd"? My love life probably. Not that I've got one yet.

I can't even read my letter from Dream Boy because I left it under my pillow in my Darkly Demanding Damson Diary.

We finished at four o'clock after jazz dance and went into the café to have a drink. It's nearly dark already. I'm going to need a torch soon to get home.

Flossie said, "Anyone fancy going down to the studios? We could make Bob let us play around doing some singing. If we pretend we really like Zep Lepplin or whoever it is he . . ."

At that point Bob walked into the café with a sign, which he hung on the wall by the door.

The sign read: *Don't bathe until further notice. Rat in tank.*

As he waddled off he hung the hammer in the back of his belt and we could definitely see his bottom crack. Flossie said, "I've sort of gone off going down to the studio."

Jo got up and said, "I think I'm going to go and . . . you know . . . read."

And she went off.

Vaisey said, "She's upset about Phil not being at the tree."

When I got back to Dandelion Cottage, I was so tired that I had my supper and went to bed even before the lunatic twins. They were making a dog out of washing-up liquid bottles and said, "For oo."

So in my bed it's me, Mr. Fevver man, and Sudsy the dog.

How many days is it until Alex the Good will be here?

I don't know what day he wrote his letter, but he said in a couple of weeks. And you would come home on a Friday, wouldn't you? So I think it will be the weekend after next.

I'm going to start my "normal topics" list. For things that are normal to talk to boys about.

I will tell you what is on the not-normal topic list.

Knees.

Spontaneous Irish dancing.

Face-licking.

Lavinia.

I know she only wants to be pretend friends with me because she likes Alex.

So what is normal?

I can't mention my home life.

Oh, I know, I can read my *A Midsummer Night's Dream* and then I could talk to him about that. I could even drop in a line casually mentioning my doing the play and how it would be good to get his ideas.

Right, here we are.

In the SparkNotes about the play it says the major themes are love's difficulty, magic, and dreams.

Spooky.

That's me and Alex.

I woke suddenly when it was still dark because I'd fallen asleep and had a nightmare. Harold had knitted me some tights and I had them on when Charlie walked into my squirrel room and said, "I've got a girlfriend. Do you want to see her?"

And he got a small blond girlfriend out of his pocket. Then Dr. Lightowler flew in, onto the top of the wardrobe, and said, "Look at her uncontrollable legs."

Then Cain and Alex came through the window and Cain said, "Show us the knees, soft lass, I feel like licking them."

I shouted, "I can dance! I can dance!"

And I tried to dance and found that Harold had knitted the legs of my tights together.

Eat the boat!

I MUST HAVE DRIFTED off to sleep properly because suddenly it was gone eight and I had to race around to get to Dother Hall in time. I put on my new yellow lacy corker holder and a yellow jumper that Georgia helped me to get.

The jummie is quite clingy.

Good. That's good. And my hair is bouncy and perky. And shiny. If I wear a skirt with dark tights it makes my legs look almost normal length. I made sure my tights weren't knitted together.

I thought everyone had gone when I went downstairs because it was all quiet. I made for the door with my breakfast banana. (I don't mean the banana was walking along with me, I just mean . . . anyway, it wasn't a walking banana.)

But then Dibdobs popped out unexpectedly from the

cupboard under the stairs.

She beamed at me.

Her beaming can be quite alarming first thing in the morning.

She blinked at me through her glasses. She is the smiliest, oddest person I have ever met. I like her though. Sadly she wasn't on her own in the cupboard.

She smiled and said, "Great news, Lullah. We started to knit the Christmas hats last night. We are hoping the whole village can have one. The twins are modeling theirs."

Max and Sam came out of the cupboard in their knitted antler hats. As she pulled them out of the door, Dibdobs said, "What color would you like, Lullah?"

I was a bit late as I ran across the green. It was overcast and looked like rain. Ruby was just setting off up the hill to her school with Matilda. Matilda had a rain hat on. Ruby saw me running and yelled over, "Ay, Loobylullah, you really jiggle when you run! Ta-ra, see you later."

I waved at her and crossed the bridge and then jogged into the woodland lane that led to Dother Hall. Or "Dither Hall" as Mr. Barraclough calls it. I am surprised that the vandal who changed *Skipley, Home of the West Riding Otter* to *Skipley, Home of the West Riding Botty* hadn't had a go at our sign.

Despite the Charlie thing, I have a song in my heart and my song is "Woo-hoo-hoo-hooo. I've got corkers and

I got a letter from a Dream Boy. Wooo-hooo-hooo, the jiggler is back in town!!!"

First thing we changed into our dance gear and went straight into the dance studio and Blaise Fox was there. She has had her hair cut into a crew cut and dyed white blond. She was dressed in silver leggings and enormous shorts.

I said to the others, "Oh no, she's got her drum."

She shouted, "Here you are again, you little minxes. And here I am, the minx mistress. And yes, you will notice I have my drum!!!!"

Monty came rushing in, well, as quickly as he could in his leotard. He was carrying a megaphone. Blaise said, "Now, girls, I know it's the second day back and we need to ease our way into things gently so we are going to do an improvised free-form version of *Jaws*."

We looked at each other. *Jaws*. The film about a killer shark that is mostly underwater? And . . .

Monty put some seaweedy-looking stuff on his head.

Blaise shouted, "Right, girls. It's a calm day and you are the sea. Feel the sea. Find your inner sea. BE the sea!"

Monty was encouraging us by scampering around in his leotard. With his seaweed head.

Jo said, "Is he a sea anemone? Or a jellyfish?"

Actually, in his pink leotard he looks more like a jellybaby.

Monty was doing a bit of light leaping. And singing,

"Wish, swish, wish, swish."

Flossie started swishing backward and forward, throwing her arms above her head. She said, "That's my foam."

Oh, well, in for a penny, in for a pound, the rest of us started doing a sort of giant hokey cokey. Pulsing in and pulsing out.

It was quite soothing. I could have done it all day. Backward and forward. Swishy swish swish. Other girls were rushing backward and forward, flapping their arms around. I didn't know that waves could do skipping, but what do I know, I was doing the hokey cokey.

Then Blaise started beating her drum.

Softly at first. *Bang-bangity-bang-bang.*

She pointed at Milly and her mates and said, "Now then, this group here, you be little children playing around in the lovely waves. Splashy splashy. Laughy laughy laughy. In amongst the swishy swishy."

This was all very pleasant and soothing for first thing in the morning.

The drumbeat started getting louder and faster.

Blaise shouted, "Tallulah, you be the shark."

What? How do you be a shark?

Blaise shouted through her megaphone, "Flossie, Vaisey, you are the boat, and Jo, you are the madman in charge. The drunken insane captain."

Flossie and Vaisey started being the boat, and Blaise was yelling through the megaphone: "Splice the mainbrace!!!

Clean the poop deck!!! MORE RUM!"

I started doing breaststroke.

Blaise said, "Oy, shark, look, no, don't look because you can't see, SNIFF . . ."

I started doing sniffing and breaststroke. Jo nearly fell overboard she was laughing so much.

Blaise said, "There's some children playing in the shallows. Start sharking toward them. Children, keep playing around and splashing, you've nothing to think about except what kind of ice cream you will have . . . la la-la, la la-la . . . You don't see the sharky yet."

Blaise was yelling at me. "You're getting a bit peckish and looking for snacks."

She and Monty started a joint impro of the theme to *Jaws* on megaphone and drum.

"Der der . . . der der . . . Come on, shark, circle nearer . . . der der, der der . . . oooooh, look at those little legs waving about . . . der der, der der . . . ooooh, one of the children has seen your fin!!!!!! They are all trying to swim and make for the shore. One of them is swimming out to sea. Quickly, quickly, your supper is escaping!!!"

I don't know what I was doing. I think it was mainly fast crawl and teeth baring.

Monty got carried away, flung down his drum, and tried to be a heroic surfer diving in to save the little children. But I gradually dismembered him. I have to say, he made an absolute meal of the whole thing. (Tee-hee, must put that in my Darkly Demanding Damson Diary.)

I had to sit on him in the end. Which is quite clever for a shark, I think. People say that sharks have brains the size of a walnut. Corker size, in fact, but . . .

I couldn't think anymore because Blaise was shouting at me: "Rear up and bite his head off!!! Eat the boat, eat the boat!!!"

Two hours of it.

I'm exhausted. Everyone's exhausted. I think Monty ripped his leotard.

And also I have a big bruise on my bum where Jo as the mad old captain stuck a mime harpoon in me.

Jo said, "Sorry about that, Tallulah—too much rum."

She doesn't know her own strength.

I'm so hot that my hair is sticking to my head. Flossie fell over a fire bucket because her fringe had glued itself to her glasses. I can't tell you how red Vaisey was. Even her curls have gone droopy.

When we staggered into the loos I glanced into the mirror—a red-faced orangutan stared back at me. Its hair plastered down to its skull. It was panting.

It was me. Mr. Sharky. Thank goodness Alex the Good can't see me now. As I supported myself against the sink, I realized I am surrounded on every side by notices from Bob.

Listen up, Dudes, forget the towel.
The towel is yesterday.
Shake your hands about a bit.

And even by the (switched-off) radiators:

Cold? You will be if the Ice Age comes again.

After I had shaken my head around to dry my hair I went into the loo. On the loo door it said:

Couldn't you hang on for a bit?

Oh phew. I was certainly feeling the bleeding slippers of fame. And maybe even the bleeding bottom of fame. I'm going to just have a look to see if I have got a bruise on my . . .

Flossie shouted, "Lullah, where are you? We are going to the sacred tree again to eat our lunch."

I said through the door, "I'm just having a little private . . ."

Flossie looked at me from under the door.

"Poo?"

"Er, no. I'm just . . ."

Then Jo's head popped up over the next cubicle.

"Come on. You're being selfish, just looking at your own bottom. I want to talk about me and whether Phil might be at the tree today."

This was ridiculous.

Vaisey's curls bobbed up next to Jo and she looked down at me and said, "My head's not so red any more, is it? Maybe the boys will be at the sacred tree. Come on, Lullah."

I was being looked at in the loo. This would have never happened at my old school.

I staggered out. Ouch, ouch!

When we got there, the boys weren't at our tree.

I said, "Come on then, let's go back."

Then we heard the barking of dogs in the distance. And coming nearer, the sound of panting and crashing through the trees.

It was really scary and for some reason we all got onto a tree stump that was about a foot high, and held on to each other. Vaisey practically had her head buried in my corker area.

The barking was getting closer and closer and so was the panting and crashing.

I said, "Maybe it's a pack of wild otters."

Jo said, "I can hear barking."

I said, "Well, a pack of barking wild otters."

Jo said, "Otters don't bark."

I said, "They do now."

Flossie said in a doomy voice, "No, no, it will be Fang

and his wild child puppies."

Noooooooooooo.

The panting and scuffling got nearer and nearer. We closed our eyes. I was so tired after being Mr. Sharky, I said, "Please don't hurt us. We mean you no harm."

The crashing stopped and a voice gasped, "Bloody hell, it's the Tree Sisters on a stump!"

Charlie.

It was Charlie, Jack, Ben, and another couple of lads we had seen about from Woolfe Academy. But no sign of Phil. Perhaps the otters had got him.

We were still on the stump while the boys flung themselves onto the ground, panting and sweaty. They had tracky bums on and vests with numbers on the front. And attached to the numbers were a couple of sausages.

Jack was getting his breath back, but then he said, "Hello, Vaisey," and he beamed at her.

She looked a bit shy and then smiled back at him. Her curls were all smiley. She's right—Jack has got a nice cheeky face. His teeth are crooked but in a good way and he's got curly hair like hers. As I was looking at him I caught Charlie's eye and he smiled.

Him with his crinkly turning-up smile. And his really nice, slightly curly, dark blond hair, and hands and legs. And so on. But then I remembered what Charlie had done to me the last time I had seen him. Swine.

Boy swine. I would give him my icy icicle treatment. I

didn't smile back at him. I just looked away.

Then Ben smiled at me. Oh yes. With his floppy hair and his bat kissing. Yeah, his bat kissing and then saying that I was too young for him. Swine. Floppy-haired swine.

All boys are swines.

They snog you and dump you. Or lick your face. Or put bats in your mouth. Apart from Alex, who wouldn't dream of licking your face and even if he did I would probably like it and, and . . .

Charlie was still panting but he said to me, "Oy, oy, Tallulah, we meet again. I've got a top view of your exceptional knees here, wrapped up in what look like dance tights. Have you got any snacks?"

I became icicle-like. I was an icicle in dance tights. I stepped down from the stump, trying to hide my knees, and said coolly, "Hello, Charles, I'm afraid I have no snacks, sadly. Why don't you eat your sausage?"

Charlie looked at me in amazement.

Vaisey said, "You've got your secret crisp stash, Lullah."

I didn't say anything.

Charlie said, "Lullah, it's me!"

Jo leapt down from the stump, threw herself into his lap, and gave him a huge hug. She said, "Charlie, Charlie. I've got a banana you can have."

Charlie gave her a big hug and took the banana.

There he goes again. Hugging. Eating people's bananas.

I know about his type.

A type that hugs a friend. (Also known as me.) And then pretends that he likes that friend's knees. And is all round friendly and huggy. And then goes from hugging to snogging. And does good knee-trembling snogging. Then stops and says, "This is wrong, I've got a girlfriend." And then goes back to his stupid pocket-sized girlfriend to hug her. Leaving a trail of hugs.

While I was wondering what to do next, Jo said, "Charlie, where's Phil? How come he's not with you? Is he in detention already?"

Charlie put his arm around her. I couldn't help it—I felt a bit jealous. Of my own pal. But Charlie, the serial hugger, is in fact very good-looking and when he smiles his mouth turns up at one side. It's a very nice shape mouth and you can actually imagine it pressing against your . . . Oh no! I have forgotten my icicle work.

Charlie hugged Jo a bit more and said in his deep voice, "Er, no, he's not in detention. He's not even at Woolfe. Phil's not coming back to Woolfe."

Jo leapt up.

"What do you mean Phil's not coming back to Woolfe??"

Oh no.

Jo's little face was all red and hot.

Her conker head was bobbing furiously.

"He didn't even tell me. Doesn't he like me anymore?

I didn't even punch him very hard and he—"

Charlie said, "It's nothing to do with that. He really does like you."

Jo looked puzzled, and like she was about to cry.

"He told me about telling the police that teenage boys are people too. And he tidied his room."

Charlie said, "Yeah, well, it got announced in assembly this morning. The headmaster at his old school has given him a second chance. For good behavior. Our headmaster, Hoppy, said he was an inspiration to us all."

Jo said, "What do you mean?"

Charlie said, "I'm so sorry to tell you this, but he's being sent back to ordinary school."

We were all shocked.

I said, "Phil . . . ordinary school? No. No, that's . . ."

Vaisey said, "It's inhuman."

We could hear the barking and shouting really near and Charlie scrambled to his feet. He had his back to me as he looked into the woods. He's got a nice bottom. Not that I think about bottoms. Or noticed his bottom particularly. It just happened to be there. Attached to his legs.

Jo was saying, "But I won't ever see him again."

Charlie hesitated.

"I can't stay now. Hoppy has organized a drag race for the beginning of term and I'm one of the foxes. We have to leave a trail of sausages so that the dogs and other boys can hunt us down."

Flossie said, "Mmmm, nice. So you boys are actually like animals in joggy bums."

The boys started to run off. Jack called to Vaisey, "See you at the gig."

And she said, "Look!" and showed him the plectrum. He gave her a thumbs-up and a big grin and he went off.

Charlie stopped as he went by me and looked me in the eyes and said quietly, "Look, Lullah . . . about that thing . . . that happened . . . well, can we . . . forget about it?"

The barking was getting very near now.

He said, "Oh, bugger it," and turned and ran off into the woods after the others.

What did "Oh, bugger it" mean in boy language?

What does "can we forget about it" mean?

As we walked back to Dother Hall, Vaisey was all flushed and said, "Jack gave me a thumbsy-up for having his plectrum."

She was all smiley.

Jo wasn't. She'd gone all floppy and miserable. She wasn't the only one. I was thinking about what Charlie had said to me about "forgetting about it."

Well, he could rely on me.

I've forgotten about "it" already. Whatever "it" is.

The show must go on. Even with a bruised bottom.

Human glue

JO WAS QUIET FOR the rest of the day, and then after last bell she disappeared.

Vaisey said, "Maybe she has gone on the roof. Like when I thought that Jack had dumped me. You know, when Cain told him about the band rules."

Oh yes, I remembered. Cain had told Jack that he couldn't go out with Vaisey because the band members of The Jones didn't have regular girlfriends. He said it was "anti-band" practice. Cain would say that.

We trooped up the stairs past the dorms and then up the narrow stairs that led on to the roof.

When we got there we discovered that Bob had put a *Danger Area—absolutely NO Admittance. Dangerous tarpaulin* notice across the stairs to the roof with a bit of ribbon to stop us going there.

Vaisey climbed over it, and me and Flossie walked straight through. Bob's not around anyway. Probably gone off to comb his bob. We had a look on the roof but apart from a flapping tarpaulin held down with bricks there was nothing up there. It was chilly and lonely. Leaning over the parapet, I could just about see the dark outline of Woolfe Academy. I thought about Charlie over there. Not thinking about the thing that he wants us to forget about.

Oh yes, I am sure he wants to forget about the thing.

Forget about snogging a person and . . . and leading that person on. And pretending to like a person's knees.

Well, I don't think I can be friends with a boy like that.

Whoever he is.

I forget.

As we went back down into the dorm, Flossie pointed at the ceiling and said to me, "That tarpaulin is the only thing between us and the sky. Vaisey found a dead pigeon on her bedside table last night, didn't you, Vaisey?"

Vaisey shook her curls around and said cheerfully, "Yeah, but it was just the one and it looked a bit depressed."

Flossie said, "Well, it would be depressed, it was dead."

Vaisey said, "No, but before that, you know, it looked like it didn't have any mates."

I said, "Let me get this right, Vaisey, are you saying that a pigeon committed suicide?"

Vaisey went a bit red. "Well, it looked upset."

"Did you find a suicide note in its beak?"

Then we noticed that the curtain round Jo's bed was drawn. We had a little peak through and Jo was lying on her bed looking at some letters. I bet they are from Phil. She looked up with her mouth all turned down like Matilda. I did my best smile, but she looked down at her letters again. Oh dear.

Flossie was rummaging through her drawers and said, "This will cheer you up, Jo. I've got some cheeky new corker holders."

She held up a polka-dot lacy bra to show me and Vaisey.

It looked a bit on the large side. We went and poked our heads through Jo's curtain. Flossie was dangling her corker holder in front of Jo. She said, "Look at these beauties."

I was still looking at Flossie's corker holder and said, "Flossie, is that the right size for you? Are you sure it fits? Isn't it a bit on the, er, large side?"

Flossie had her Deep South accent on again and said, "Oh, it fits all right, Tallllluuuuulah Casey. It fits REAL fine. Real snug! I'll show you." And she went off and swished the curtain round her bed.

I sat on Vaisey's bed next to Jo's curtain and said, "Are you okeydokey, my little friendette, do you want to arm wrestle or something? You like that."

There was a pause and then Jo's voice came through sounding like she was under a blanket. She said, "What if

I never see him again? He's the first boy I've ever kissed."

Then from behind her curtain Flossie said, "Why, sometimes on hooootttt nights, I'm just a-setting on the stoop to get some air . . . or is it stooping on the set? I can't rightly say. I don't know what ah do, it's so goddam hooootttttt. Hey, open a window, y'all."

Fat chance. It was about minus fifty, and anyway, you can't open the windows because mostly there aren't any. It's just frames covered in clingfilm. Another Bob DIY job to cut costs. This whole place is falling down.

Jo said from behind her curtain, "I knew he was too short in the first place. When I first saw him, I said, didn't I? I should never have trusted him. You can't trust short people. Look at clowns."

I was going to have to be firm to be kind with her.

I went and pulled back the curtain.

I said, "Look, Jo, well, not to, you know, upset your applecart and so on, but you yourself are quite . . . you are quite, you know."

I patted her head.

She said, "Why are you patting my head?"

I looked down at her as she looked up at me. I said, "Well, you know, because I can."

Her face went all dark and red. I stepped back.

She said, "Are you saying I'm short?"

I said, "Well, no, I'm just saying that shortness is not

a reason not to trust people. There're lots of other reasons not to trust them, but . . ."

Jo wasn't listening, she was just getting redder. She stood up on her bed and looked me in the eyes and said, "Maybe I am a normal size and you are a giant girl with . . . with . . . big nobbly legs!!"

Oh, that was a bit mean.

Jo drew the curtains around her bed again really violently. Huh.

Vaisey had been lying down kicking her legs about when she sat up and said, "I think Jack might like me still, don't you? He smiled at me a lot, didn't he, and said 'see you at the gig'? And he gave me the thumbs-up when I waved the plectrum, didn't he? It was a proper smile, wasn't it? Crinkly. You'll come to The Jones's gig with me on Saturday, won't you, Lullah?"

I said, "Well, I—"

Flossie flung back her curtain and came cavorting out in her new bra and pants.

Crikey and yikes!

She walked up and down in front of Vaisey and me, swinging her hips around and shaking her corker holder. Still speaking in her ridiculous Southern drawl.

"Phew. It just gets so damn hoooootttttt in October in Yorkshire that I often walk about in mah underwear . . . just like those goddam Brontë sisters."

Vaisey said, "If Bob comes in now his bob will fall off."

I said, "Flossie. Have you got stuff in that bra that's not you?"

She said, "Why, Miss Lullah, you just talk so much silly talk."

Vaisey said, "You do seem much more sticky-outy than you did before you went behind the curtain."

Flossie said, "Well, it's the goddam heat, it just makes everything grow like crazee."

I went and pulled out two pairs of tights from her corker holder.

Flossie said, "Well, I never, how in God's name did they git in there?"

It made us laugh. Well, most of us.

I said, "Jo, come and look at this!"

There was silence from behind Jo's curtain.

And a tiny soft snuffling.

And then more snuffling.

Oh no.

I looked at the others, then I said through the curtain, "Jo, do you remember that Phil said you were a cracking snogger?"

Jo's muffled voice said, "So?"

I said, "Well, my cousy said that if you have excellent snogging skills, it's like . . . human glue."

No, she hadn't said that.

Where had "human glue" come from?

I am a genius. I must write "human glue" in my Darkly Demanding Damson Diary.

After a bit of silence, Jo said, "What do you mean, human glue?"

Ah.

Well.

Good point.

I didn't have a clue what I meant by human glue.

But, hellfire, I was on the brink of a showbiz career. I'd been a shark this morning. I had the scars to prove it. I could improvise. "Aaah, I'm glad you brought that up."

Vaisey and Flossie looked at me. Flossie started dancing with her teddy-bear pajama case and Vaisey got out her plectrum.

Jo drew back her curtain and looked at me.

I shook my hair dramatically and said, "Because when you are a good snogging match, everything works out all right in the end. Because you are sort of glued at the mouth."

Jo smiled and said, "Really?"

Crikey.

Back in my squirrel room I wrote in my Damson Diary:

Human glue.

I tried to remember what Cousin Georgia had said about the snogging scale. Had she said anything about glue? I know Number 1 was "holding hands," Number 2 was "arm around," Number 3 was "good-night kiss." What was Number 4 then?

Oh, I know, "a kiss lasting three minutes without a break."

But where did tongues come in? Number 5? Number 6? When bat boy Ben attacked me with his tongue, we definitely hadn't done a kiss lasting over three minutes without a break. So how come he just plunged in with his bat tongue?

He can't know the snogging scale.

And Cain hadn't even bothered with Number 1 before he . . .

Oh, I don't know.

Calf love

HONEY IS ARRIVING TODAY. I'm so excited. She's lovely and also sort of more experienced. She knows a lot about boys. I wonder what number she's got to? I was panting a bit because I'd been walking really fast, and so leaned for a minute on the fence by the road that turned off to Woolfe Academy.

When I next see Charlie, I'm going to be very icicle-like with him.

I will be cool friendly, not rude but just cool, and forgetting about "it," whatever "it" is I am supposed to be forgetting about. I've forgotten "it" already.

Then I nearly died of a heart attack because the girls popped out from behind a fence with their umbrellas up, like three mad Mary Poppins.

I shouted, "Jesus, Joseph, and Mary!!!!!"

And they all laughed. Vaisey said, "Guess who's here!"

Honey popped up from behind the fence.

She was sooo excited.

"Loobbyyluuuullah!!!! Ooohhhh, it's WEALLY WEALLY gweat to see you!!!!" And she came over and hugged me. Then we all started hugging. And jumping up and down.

She's just the same, sooo Honeyish. Not in a sticky way, just smoothy and golden and sweet. So pretty and with lovely golden hair and quite curvy. When she let go of me for a minute I looked at her properly.

She had an amazing mink-colored suede miniskirt and jacket on. And long boots to match. And her hair looked sort of "done."

I said, "Hey, have you got false eyelashes on?"

She smiled and said, "Yeth, they awe weally natuwal, don't you think?"

And she blinked a lot so we could all see.

I said, "I'm going to get some."

Honey said, "Aww, Looby, you don't need to, your eyeth are all gweeney and like a cat'th eyeth."

I felt a little smile turning my mouth up at the corners, first the jiggling corkers and now the cat's eyes. Life was good. Even as a boy reject. I said modestly, "Oh, eyes-smyes, they're just a bit green, you know. Nothing unusual about that. Loads of people have green eyes."

Vaisey said, "No, they don't, it's mostly brown."

I said, "Oh really? Yes, I suppose it is. People have, you know, noticed my eyes are quite green. Cat's eyes they said as well. Yes, there is a boy and he calls me Green Eyes so I suppose that must mean that they really are green and not just . . . brown."

Flossie said, "Lullah, have you ever heard the expression 'Shut up about your eyes'? Yes, they are nice, but just shut up about it now."

I looked at her and said, "You can't stop me."

She said, "I can."

And I said, "I know."

She shook my hand.

We linked up as we walked along. Wow, proper friends, I've got proper friends. The Tree Sisters. And it has stopped raining. We put our umbies down and Vaisey said, "We're like the Brontë sisters on a good day."

I couldn't help thinking that Chaz, Em, and Anne didn't ever have good days. Unless you count the day they got an extra turnip, and Em wrote about it in *Wuthering Turnips*.

Even Jo was leaping up and down like an excitable retriever. It was my pep talk about human glue kissing that did it. I am quite wise in the ways of boys. Even though I don't know what I am talking about.

Jo was shaking Honey.

"Tell her! Tell Lullah what you told us, tell her the news!! Go on!!!"

Vaisey said, "You won't believe it, Lullah, you really won't."

What was going on?

Flossie said, "It's incWEDIBLE!! Isn't it, Honey?"

Honey smiled and said, "Well, actually it weally ith."

And it really was. Honey has been, what do you call it? Talent spotted!

Vaisey's curls were bobbing about all over the shop. She said, "By an American-type person. Not from here or anything. A Hollywood-type of person. With a cigar."

Honey said, "He came to see me in *West Side Stowy* over the holiday and he weally liketh my thinging and evewything and he wanths me to be in movieth. I don't weally know why he liketh me tho much, but . . ."

I gave her a big hug and I said, "It's because you've got a lovely voice and you're just, you know, lovely all over."

She hugged me back. And I could feel her corkers against mine. And that made me go a bit red. And tingly.

Honey noticed too because she looked down at my corker area.

I stopped the hugging and folded my arms in front of me.

As we walked on, she said, "Yeth, so I'll be flying off to do some scween testth."

I said, "But Honey, why did you come back here at all, why didn't you just go to Hollywood?"

"I wanted to be with my fwends and to say good-bye PWOPOLY."

Oooohhhhh. That was so nice. Awwwww. She deserved a hugging for that.

And we all did another spontaneous hug. Holy moly, I have become a multi-spontaneous hugger. I am turning into Dibdobs.

We were still hugging and squealing when suddenly Charlie came out of the undergrowth. His hair was wet and he had a waterproof on. He still managed to look cool though.

Unlike me probably. I hoped my skirt hadn't ridden up over my tights while I was doing free-form hugging.

Charlie laughed when he saw us and did his smile. He caught my eye but I looked down at the floor.

"Aha, you're here, the Tree Sisters. Nice to see you, Honey."

She fluttered her false eyelashes at him and said in her deep honeyed voice, "It's weally nice to see you ath well, Chawie."

Charlie looked hypnotized and then quickly said, "I hoped I might find you. Can I join in?"

And Charlie came and leapt into our hugging circle next to me. He had his arm around me and I'm sure it was his hand on my bottom. I'd had a boy's hand on my bottom before, one of Connor's mates, but he had pretended it wasn't his hand, it was him resting his rucksack.

Charlie didn't have a rucksack.

How am I supposed to do icicle work under these circumstances?

His face was so close to mine I could feel his warm breath on my cheek.

I swished my hair so that it fell down and shielded my face.

He said, "Well, this is cozy, girls."

Everyone laughed. And he laughed. He's got a nice laugh. And he smells nice, not like Connor, who mostly smells of socks and hamster. I think that Charlie washes himself. And also he might wear boy perfume. I couldn't stand the tension of being so near to him. My knees were tensing. Oh no, not Irish dancing.

Then, thank goodness, just before I started leaping around or neighing or something, Honey said, "Chawlie, I'm going to Hollywood!!!"

Charlie let go of me and said to her, "Wow, Honey, how fab is that, you little star."

And he gave her a big hug. For slightly too long, I thought. Honey didn't try to get away either.

Charlie just can't seem to stop hugging. He is a serial hugger.

And then it got worse. If Charlie had been hugging me, especially in front of everyone, I would have either done my spontaneous Irish dancing or Tourette syndrome of the leg as some people might call it. Or gone unconscious.

But Honey didn't go unconscious. She went femme fatale. I had seen her do it before on Ben and his head had practically dropped off. She looked down and then she looked up and looked Charlie straight in the eyes. And she was slightly smiling. And fluttering her false eyelashes up and down. Crumbs, she was going the whole hog. She touched her lips with her fingers, kissed them, and then she put her fingers that she had kissed on his lips and said softly, "Oh, Chawlie, I'll mith you."

It was like being in a French film. Possibly. I don't know, I've never seen one. But my grandma said the French were "always at it."

Charlie cleared his throat and leaned down toward her. I thought he was going to snog her! But he kissed her on the cheek and said, "I'll miss you too, pet."

I was thinking, "Oh yes, you'll miss her, if you've got time in between all the other girls that you might miss or you've got in your pocket or . . ."

But then he moved away from her and said to all of us, "Look, girls, I would love to stay around hugging with you all day but we've got hopping practice. And I actually came to see Jo because I got a phone call from Phil last night."

We looked at Jo and she went bright red. She looked a bit frightened as well. What next? Charlie went on, "He says can you make it to the public phone in the village, round the corner from The Blind Pig on Saturday at seven?"

Jo stuttered, "Well, I, er . . . well, I, er . . ."

As he turned to go off, he looked back at me and said, "Tallulah, we need to talk about stuff."

And he was gone.

The others looked at me.

Flossie said, "What was that about, Tallulah? What stuff?"

Honey said, "I think he might like you, Tallulah. He ith thooooo gorguth. You should go out with him. I would. Why don't you?"

I shrugged and was just about to think of something to say when Jo started hitting tree trunks with her bag.

"Oh, it's all about Tallulah's knees! Or Tallulah's corkers. Or talking or something! Shut up about Tallulah, what about me? This is about me! Phil is going to phone me!!!"

And she started doing run-run-leap around us. Then we heard the assembly bell ring in the distance and we all tore off up the drive to Dother Hall.

We went on running through the main doors, into the cloakroom, running on the spot as we took our coats off and then ran straight into the main hall.

I wish I knew why we were running.

We'd just scrabbled to our seats panting and were doing sitting-down running on the spot because we were so excited, when the stage door opened and Dr. Lightowler appeared. I stopped my legs immediately and got them under control.

Dr. Lightowler said, "Settle down, girls," and swished her cloak about. It was made of black velvet and looked like it had fun fur on the inside.

I said quietly to Jo, "She's grown a winter cloak."

Even though you would have had to be a dog to hear me, her beady eyes swiveled round and fixed on me. And not in a good way. Not in a "hello, Tallulah, how lovely to see you" way.

"And when I say settle down, girls, I particularly mean you, Tallulah Casey."

Jo said, "Boy, does she hate you."

I don't know why she does. It's something about my legs. She thinks I have grown them extra long just to annoy her. And that I do Irish dancing on purpose. She doesn't know about having Tourettes of the legs.

Dr. Lightowler went on, "The principal is away on urgent business today. In the meantime, as you know, our winter project is a reworking of *A Midsummer Night's Dream* and I expect you all to fully participate. Keeping notebooks, doing lunchtime performances, etc. I don't think all of you understand the great honor it is to be at Dother Hall. But can I remind you that this is not Liberty Hall. You have come to work. And work hard. Those of you not up to the mark may well find yourselves, quite literally, as in the Bard's play, being Bottom."

What is she talking about? And why is she looking at me?

Monty and Gudrun were trumpeting with laughter at "being Bottom." In fact, Gudrun got hiccups and had to leave the hall.

It was only half-past nine in the morning and I was already tired. And confused. Having my bottom felt by a serial hugger and then the serial hugger saying, "we need to talk about stuff."

What did "we need to talk" mean? What does "stuff" mean?

We need to talk about forgetting about stuff? What was stuff?

For our first lesson, Monty turned up with a copy of *A Midsummer Night's Dream* and wearing green corduroy trousers to the knee and a cap with a feather in it. He said, "Girls, good morning, and especially good morning to Honey. Welcome, my dear, welcome back. I hope to hear your lovely voice in our production. Perhaps as the Queen of the Fairies?"

Honey smiled at him in her Honey way. But when she looked round at me, she looked a bit sad. She won't be in *A Midsummer Night's Dream,* she will be riding around in a limo in a Hollywood dream.

Monty went to sit down on a table but his trousers were too tight to bend easily, so he put one arm on the top of the table and leaned back, in a casual storytelling pose.

He said, "Once more we enter the magical, tragical, comedical world of Shakespeare and his wondrous fairy tale. Now, as you may know, a great deal of the action takes place in the woods and to get into the proper spirit we shall ourselves, 'enter the woods.' The woods are of course a metaphor for the imagination and subconscious."

Rain started pelting against the windows.

I said to the others, "I hope he is being 'metaphorical' in that he means we will enter the woods in our minds, but not actually have to go outside into the howling rain."

Honey said, "I don't want to spoil my bootth, the wain might wuin them for Hollywood. I don't think they will like thoggy bootth in Hollywood."

Flossie said, "I know, and my pants are only just dry from yesterday. I put them on the dorm radiator to dry. If Bob had found them I would have been hung for offenses against the planet."

Everyone else seemed keen to get into the woods.

Vaisey said, "Come on, it will be fun." And stuffed her curls into her hat.

Monty started putting on his raincoat. My coat was still damp from walking to Dother Hall, but who said the ladder to the stars was going to be dry? We squelched across the sodden grass and into the dripping woods. A big raindrop went right down my neck. At least no one licked it off.

Monty had his theatrical welligogs on (stars all over

them) and bustled along in front of us breathing in the damp forest air as if it was tincture of joy. Then he darted off suddenly and hid behind a tree.

We looked at each other—had we started the avant garde performance already? Then Monty's head popped out and he put his hand to his ear and said, "Sssshhhhhh. Can you begin to feel it, girls? Do you feel the magic working, girls? 'What angel wakes me from my flowery bed?' OOOohhhh, the Bard, the Bard! Genius genius!!!"

We blundered on while he yelled over his shoulder, "You can smell fairies out here!!"

We looked at each other.

Then he stopped and gasped, "Look, girls, look. Drink in the sight."

He pointed to some moldy old hawthorn berries clinging on to a twig for dear life against the wind and rain. He gazed at them as if he was about to burst into tears and clapped his hands and said, "Two lovely berries molded on one stem." And went chuckling off farther into the woods.

After about ten minutes it stopped raining and as we lagged behind things began to look quite familiar. And then we realized that he was making for our special tree place.

How did he know about it?

Honey said, "Pwaps the twee weally does have stwange powers?"

Well, it certainly had a big effect on Monty. He threw

down his satchel and began skipping round the tree.

"Girls, join in, join hands, join our little fairy throng. Let us make play in the woods, in the green woods."

We started shuffling around the tree in our raincoats.

"Lightly, girls, lightly, as if you had wings!"

So we did light skipping.

Then he said, "Now, let us talk in fairy language!"

I said, "What if the Woolfe boys come along and see us talking in high-pitched voices and skipping?"

Flossie said, "Well, they've seen us wiggling around in front of trees before."

Monty pursed his lips and started trilling in a tiny tinkling voice. I happened to be next to him in the skipping circle, holding his pudgy hand, and as we skipped he turned to me and tinkled, "Heeeeee . . . weeee . . . meeeee. Hewwww."

And he looked at me all blinky as if expecting something. Flossie, Vaisey, Jo, and the rest had their mouths puckered up. So through my pursed lips I squeaked out in my fairy voice, "Hiddddiddddleeeee didddleeee diddillleeee."

Flossie had a coughing fit she was laughing so much.

After half an hour, Jo went up to Monty and said, "Mr. de Courcy, I can't feel my bottom anymore. Can we go in?"

Monty patted her head. Uh-oh. If I was him I wouldn't have done that. Jo accidentally stepped on Monty's foot, quite hard. Then started walking back to Dother Hall.

As we followed her, Monty, slightly hopping, was still in his Shakespeare mood. He gestured after Jo and said, "She was a vixen when she went to school, and though she be but little, she is fierce."

And trilled with laughter.

As we came out of ballet class that afternoon, I said to Vaisey, "It's not really fair, is it? You know, ballet for people with my legginess. I mean, if I made Jo do, er . . . reaching for things on top shelves that wouldn't be fair on her, would it? Because she's too short to reach. So that is my point about me and ballet."

Vaisey said, "I know what you mean, but reaching up to shelves isn't on our syllabus, is it?"

And we headed up to the dorm.

We were sitting on Vaisey's bed and Jo was lying on me kicking her legs, complaining. "It's all right for you, Tallulah, all you've got to be worried about is your legs. Phil might be phoning up so that he can dump me."

Vaisey said, "Why would he do that, he could just not bother getting in touch."

Honey said, "I think he weally liketh you, Jo, he even liked you when you hit him and jumped on him."

Jo wasn't convinced.

"Yeah, but maybe he really did mind and he just didn't

say he minded, but he was storing up minding into a big fat pile of mindiness. To tell me about on the phone."

Her mood was very catching. I said, "Who knows what boys think anyway? I mean, why would anyone lick your nose? I don't remember that on Cousin Georgia's snogging scale. And do you know why? Because it's not on there."

Flossie said, "What is on the scale?"

I told them all I could remember. Up to a kiss lasting over three minutes.

Honey said, "After that it's tongueth."

We looked at her. She swished her hair about.

Vaisey said, "Tongues? At the same time? What, his tongue and your tongue?"

Honey nodded. "Well, weally you have to impwovise."

I said, "Yes, but how do you improvise if you haven't got anyone to improvise with? Ruby said that some boys were so rubbish at kissing that they should practice on something. Maybe we could do that. You know, improvise with something."

Flossie said, "Like what?"

"Well, Ruby suggested balloons."

They just stared.

Jo said, "What if you accidentally bit the balloon?"

"Why would you accidentally bite a balloon?" I said.

Honey said, "You can do a bit of a pwactice by using one of your fwends' legth."

★ ★ ★

When it was my turn to practice, I put my lips on Flossie's calf and Honey said, "Wight, Lullah, try sticking your tongue out just a little bit and sort of darting it in and out."

So I did. Even though I can't really imagine when I am going to be kissing someone's calf. But what do I know?

Then Flossie started groaning and going, "Oooooh, that is so damn good. Why I declare, Miss Tallulah, you're making me feel sooooo gooooood."

It was horrific.

In the end, I stopped doing it on the back of Flossie's leg, because she was doing her Texan accent and it made me feel sort of dirty.

It was better with Honey, but she said I was too tickly, I have to practice more even pressure apparently.

Oooooh, I wish my Dream Boy was here to rescue me. I bet I could get my pressure right with him.

I wanted to go straight up to my squirrel room when I got home. I didn't feel like hugging or eating anything local, so I said to Dibdobs I had homework to do.

She said, "Oooooh, I bet you are going to be a big superstar, with your lovely long legs and your oooooooohh-hhh gorgeousness. Isn't she gorgeous, boys? Isn't Tallulah gorgeous? With her legs and everything?"

And so I found myself in a hugging extravaganza anyway. And I've got a local sausage in each hand.

As I lie here, cuddling my squirrel slipper and Hammy

and eating my sausages, I so wish I had a boyfriend to help me and to talk to. Someone sort of older and more, well, more Alex-shaped. I've been practicing my signature for the letter I'm going to write to him.

I don't like to ask Ruby if she knows when Alex will be back. She rolls her eyes if I even mention his name. Maybe I could stroll over there and not mention Dream Boy, just sort of see if I could use my feeling talents, or see if anyone accidentally mentioned him. I may as well.

Dibdobs has gone knitting with the boys. As I passed the village hall, I heard the needles clacking. There's a notice: *ARE YOU A KNIT WIT? COME ALONG AND KNIT WITH US!* next to the poster for The Jones's gig.

When I got to The Blind Pig I saw Beverley Bottomly coming out of the shop eating a doughnut. She looked at me and then she pointed two fingers to her eyes, and then pointed the fingers at my eyes and then she went off backward pointing the fingers at her eyes and then mine. Why is she doing that?

As she went off down the road she called out, "Ay, Lady Muck. I've got my eyes on you. Think on. Leave our lads alone. Or else."

Ruby was on her way out to dog obedience classes with Matilda. I'd forgotten she still goes. She's been going since summer. I can't say that it seems to make much difference to Matilda's obedience skills.

Ruby said, "Last week we did 'heel,' didn't we,

Matilda? She is right good at it. Tha knows when you say to your dog 'heel' and it comes and walks behind thee? Like this. I'll show thee what we've learned. Let's show Tallulah what you can do, Matilda. Watch, Lullah."

She took Matilda onto the green and shouted at her, "Right then. Here we go. Heel!! Matilda, heel!"

Ruby slapped her side and shouted, "Heel!!!"

Matilda put her head on one side and looked at Ruby. Ruby said, "Good girl, HEEL!"

And Matilda lay on her tummy with her legs all splayed out. Like a grilled chicken. With fur on. And a collar with a big bow on it. And looked with her moony eyes at us.

Ruby shouted, "You daft lummox, I said 'heel' not 'hoof.'" She stamped her foot and said, "She's as much use as a chocolate teapot—that's what she does when she wants a hoofy treat. Come on, Matilda."

And she went and grumpily picked Matilda up and put her over her shoulder. As she stamped off she called back, "Is tha going to The Jones's gig? It's definitely on. I saw that Seth, and he said they were going to do it. Even though Ruben and Cain aren't talking. I bet it will be brilliant. There might be a reight big fight."

And she went off whistling.

I couldn't just hang around without having her as my excuse but as no one was about I had a quick look through the pub door. No sign of Alex. Thank goodness Mr. Barraclough was out because . . . just as I was thinking that, he appeared in his pinnie.

He said in a "kindly" tone, "Now then, young man, what can I do for thee?"

I said, "Er, well, Mr. Barraclough, I am just—"

"You've got very long hair for a lad. What is it you want?"

I said, "I was just looking . . . around."

Ted looked at me.

"I know what you've come for my lad, well, as it happens I have got a photo, I'll just get it for thee."

And he went off into the pub.

How did he know? How did he know I wanted to see a photo of Alex? Had Ruby said something? Oh no.

Mr. Barraclough came back, carrying a photo.

"There you are, my fine fellow me lad, feast your eyes on that beauty."

And he handed me a publicity shot of his band. The Iron Pies.

There were four of them. And Mr. Barraclough was the smallest. It looked like the drummer would never be able to get out from behind his drums ever again.

They were all in leather and Viking helmets.

There was nothing to do but go back to my squirrel home. Dibdobs and the twins and Harold were on the sofa and they all had their feet in a big woolly thing.

I said, "Um, night-night, I'm off to bed to read *A Midsummer Night's Dream*."

Harold said, "We're experimenting with a uni-sock, Lullah, and making earmuffs. But you get about your art, *A Midsummer Night's Dream* aahhhh, 'To sleep perchance to dream.'"

It had stopped snowing. Now it was raining. The rain was tumbling down so hard, it was rattling the roof and occasionally the black sky lit up with lightning.

I started flicking through *A Midsummer Night's Dream*.

It has to be said, it is a bonkers play. All about fairies and Bottom and love potions. I'm going to write some inspirational quotes in my Darkly Demanding Damson Diary.

I write:

Nay faith, let me not play a woman. I have a beard coming!!!!!

This is a good one:

"Bless thee, Bottom!"

How hilarious to have a character called Bottom.

Oh and this reminds me of what Ted Barraclough said to Ecclesiastica Bottomly, when she was sitting on his wall:

"Methought I was enamored of an ass."

Tee-hee, imagine being called Bottomly and having such a big bottom.

Don't forget your Bottom

SIDONE WAS BACK AT assembly the next day. She came on in a gold catsuit and began pacing up and down. Like a gold cat. In a suit.

"Let me tell you a story, girls."

She came to the front of the stage and continued in a sort of softy voice, looking out like she could see something we couldn't see.

"In the heady days of my youth, I was in a Broadway production. Ealing Broadway. It was just a small part as a tomato in the çomedy, *Have You Seen My Tomatoes?*

"But I gave it my all. Every night I turned up and I BECAME a tomato. As the show went on for weeks, some of the other girls in the chorus grew tired of being tomatoes, they said the costumes made them look fat, some of them didn't even bother to dye their heads green. But I always did. Because I cared. I've always cared, perhaps I've cared just too darned much."

She looked down for ages, then she shook her shoulders and said, "I even spent most of one afternoon in a greenhouse full of tomatoes to really pick up their tomatoiness. And, girls, my girls, it paid off because one night a producer came along and saw me and plucked me from the vegetable patch and . . . and the rest is history. I lived my dream and then I came here to let others live their dreams."

At which point she smiled. That was a bit spooky.

She said, "And let us live the dream while we still can because one of our own little stars has been favored by the gods of showbiz. Has been plucked from the vegetable patch . . . Honey is off to Hollywood!!!!!!"

Everybody went mad when they heard about Honey. Lifting her up and dancing about with her. Then putting her on the stage. Her golden honey hair was shaking and curling about, and her corkers looked quite jolly as well.

When we stopped clapping and whistling, she looked out at us and said, "Oh, thank you, itth weally thweet of you to be tho glad for me, and even if I do well and they like me I will weally, weally mith you all. I will never forget Dother Hall and my fwends and teachers here. And I will come back and visit and see you all again."

Everyone clapped up a storm. I felt like crying. Monty was crying. So was Gudrun and even Bob blew his nose on his T-shirt.

Sidone glided across in her catsuit and put her arm around Honey's shoulders and spoke over the top of the hubbub. "Yes go, Honey, go fly to your dream. Live your dream. These fleeting moments of happiness amidst the interminable agony of grim despair. And loss of dreams. Say farewell, Honey, say farewell to Dother Hall. Because dreams come to an end. And then nightmares become dreams and the dreams that you dreamed are no longer dreams you can dream they are the nightmares that you dreamed were dreams."

What was she on about?

I said, "Has she snapped?"

As we looked at her everyone went silent. Sidone stretched both arms out to us and said, "My girls, my poor girls . . . my . . . poor . . . girls." Her shoulders were heaving.

And then she collapsed in a heap.

Monty rushed over to Sidone and was slapping her about the face. Then he started tugging at her arm and Blaise and Bob came on and they took an arm and a leg each and began dragging her to the side of the stage. Like she was some golden fish fingers.

Dr. Lightowler came striding on to the stage and said, "Clear the auditorium, girls. Ms. Beaver has lightly fainted. Move along quickly; she needs peace and quiet."

We shuffled out. What was going on?

Flossie said, "Madame Frances was carted off to the

loony bin last term, now Sidone this term. It's the curse of Dother Hall."

I said, "Maybe her catsuit was too tight and it . . ."

The girls were all looking at me.

"And it cut . . . off . . . the blood to her . . . head."

As we went out into the front hall the whole school was talking about Sidone fainting. What did she mean about dreams becoming nightmares and "my poor girls, my poor girls"?

Bob was bobbing about taking down one of his environmental notices.

I said, "Has global warming finished then, Bob? I thought it was getting a bit colder."

He didn't even look at us, just hitched his jeans up to nearly cover the crack in his bottom and said gloomily, "My next job will be boarding up the windows."

Vaisey said, "Why would you do that, how would we see out?"

Bob said, "You won't see out because you won't be here. If Sidone can't pay the taxman we're all out of here. On the road again."

The atmosphere at Dother Hall was weird for the rest of the week. We saw Sidone, dressed in black, huddled in corners with Monty, Dr. Lightowler, and Gudrun. Looking very serious. Sometimes shaking a sad handkerchief at us as we passed. Even Blaise Fox seemed not her usual self. It didn't stop her banging her drum though.

We couldn't believe that Dother Hall might close.

Flossie said, "I'm not leaving. We could chain ourselves to the fence."

I said, "There isn't a fence. Bob made it into swords for theatrical fencing class."

We were all worried though.

On my way home on Friday I was just going out of the front doors of Dother Hall when I bumped into Blaise. She was about to get into her sports car and had enormous goggles on. Which she didn't remove as I spoke to her. It seems that everyone who stays around here gradually turns into an owl.

I said to her, "Ms. Fox, can I ask you, why did Ms. Beaver faint, and why is Bob saying that if she can't pay the taxman we won't be here? Is it true that Dother Hall might close?"

I thought she was going to say, "Shut up, you fool." But she didn't.

She said, "Hmmm, well, it's not looking too good. We are going to know more on Monday, so try not to worry until then. Fling yourself around like a fool, that will cheer you up."

And she revved up her engine and tore off down the drive.

I moped about it all the way down to Heckmondwhite.

It's only half-past eight but I'm in bed looking through my diary at my ideas.

It's probably pointless keeping it anyway if Dother Hall closes and I have to go back to a non-showbiz life. Blimey, just when you think that you are growing into your knees and climbing the ladder of showbiz, some fool comes and snatches away the ladder.

If I leave Heckmondwhite, I will never see Alex the Good again. I can't leave. Something has to happen.

What did Harold say, "To sleep perchance to dream"?

If I go to sleep, perchance I will dream, perchance I will dream up a way to save Dother Hall.

That night I did dream. I was onstage at Dother Hall and the spotlight was on me. I smiled at the audience and a ripple of anticipation ran through the ranks of people. I said, "Last term I gave you my rendition of Sugar Plum Bikey, which had a few technical difficulties. However this year I would like to give you my interpretation of a flying scene by Titania, Queen of the Fairies. It's from *A Midsummer Night's Dream*, done with the aid of a rope and harness, which Bob has kindly agreed to operate."

Bob, dressed all in black, appeared from offstage. He

said, "Ladies and gentlemen, this is a special effect I perfected on tour with Zep. The arena tour from the eighties. It is a rock-and-roll masterpiece."

He went offstage and the music began. I was hauled elegantly into the air by my harness (cunningly concealed in my fairy costume). Bob was huffing and puffing on the other end of the rope. I waggled my wings delicately and sang, "Lalalalalala, I am queen of the fairies."

A dashing Oberon-like figure, I think it may have been Alex, shouted out, "Ah, my queen, well met by moonlight!!!"

I smiled at him as I adjusted my crown and wings. This time my ballet dress would not stick in the spokes of my bike. And catapult me through the fire curtains and into the backstage area. I knew this for a fact because I was not on a bike.

Vaisey, Jo, and Flossie were also dressed as fairies, and Honey as Puck started singing, "Isn't she lovely!! Isn't she wonderful?"

I was flying, I was gliding, my feet slightly off the ground, to give the impression of flight. The audience gasped at the beauty of it all. Oberon blew me a kiss. I blew him one back, thereby doing one-hand flying. It was so lovely.

Then a cry went up from somewhere offstage: "Don't forget your Bottom!!!" and Dr. Lightowler in her cloak leapt onto the stage with a massive Dumbo the Elephant head. It had long floppy ears and a trunk. She shoved the Dumbo head over mine and I couldn't see a thing.

I heard the audience gasp. As I was struggling to get the Dumbo head off, I started twirling round and round on the end of the rope. I was dizzy. I didn't know where I was. I heard a voice shout, "Mind the wall, Dumbo!!"

Blinded, I crashed into the side wall and the whole of Dother Hall started to shake and fall down.

My corkers are on the move

I WOKE UP TO discover that I had gone blind. Oh noooooo. It was only when I sat up that I remembered I'd put two slices of cucumber on my eyes overnight to make them sparkly for The Jones's gig.

At this rate it might be the last gig I go to before I have to go back to Ireland. And my old life as a lanky fool.

Still, it had stopped raining. I can't worry about every little thing.

About why Dr. Lightowler hates me and why she would put a Dumbo head on me.

Or about whether Dother Hall is going to stay open.

Or what Charlie means by "stuff."

Or whether my corkers have grown overnight.

Hang on, I can worry about that, I'm going to measure.

Oh yes!!!!! Thirty inches and a third. Yippeeee . . . hang on a minute. It's three days since I last measured so that means they are growing a third of an inch every three days. If they keep growing like this, I'll have to be airlifted out of bed.

And how do they know to grow evenly?

Perhaps they don't.

Maybe I should measure each one separately. I don't want one being eight extra inches and one being only four inches.

I wish I had never started this now.

But, hey, I am here in Brontë country. This is not the place for having weak knees. This is the place for big, red sturdy knees. I don't remember anything in *Jane Eyre* about her worrying about her corkers. In fact, I don't think she even mentioned them. She was probably as worried as I am, but she didn't mention it. Too many other things to worry about, like starvation and her husband imprisoning his first wife in the attic and then setting fire to himself.

I can learn something from Em, Chazza, and Anne. I will display Northern grit.

I washed and blow-dried my hair and made it va-va-voom. I feel better already.

As I was doing some practice swishing, Dibdobs shouted up the stairs, "See you later, Tallulah! We're going to look for more volunteer knitters."

And the door slammed.

I went down to the kitchen. Through the side window, I could see Dibdobs and the lunatic twins talking to people on the green. I saw Mrs. Wombwell hiding behind the church wall when she saw the Dobbinses approaching. I knew how she felt.

I wonder who will go to The Jones's gig? I'm only going because Vaisey wants to see Jack so much. And Jo wants us Tree Sisters to give her moral support while she waits for Phil's phone call. I am a very good pal actually because I have no reason to go. And in fact I would rather not go. I haven't seen Cain since the nose-licking thing and I don't want to.

I wonder if any of the Woolfe boys will go? Will Charlie be there?

I was having a lie down on my squirrel bed while my face mask (homemade, egg white and curry powder . . . well, I thought it might give my skin a bit of a tanned glow, it was quite orange colored) took hold and worked its magic. I was planning how icy and cool I was going to be if Charlie did turn up. And wanted to "talk."

Oh, I bet I can guess what he wants to "talk" about, probably how much he really likes his girlfriend and can we just be friends. Yeah, well, friends don't do snogging and hugging, do they?

I won't say that though. I will just look at him and nod. Icily. So he doesn't really know what my nod means. But he will know I am being icy.

In all honesty, after I have punished him with my icy nod, I would quite like to be friends with him. Even after being so upset. It would be nice to have a boy matey mate. Maybe he could help me understand how boys work? He might even be able to help me with Alex.

I went to run a bath and heard the sound of a stone being thrown against my window.

It was Ruby with Matilda. She looked up and said, "Bloody Nora, tha looks like a pillock."

I said, "Thanks for that, Ruby."

"Hey, you will nivver guess what, there might be trouble at The Jones's gig toneet. I can't wait. All the village girls are saying that you Dother Hall lot are stuckup Lady Mucks that are stealing their lads."

What?

She was hopping up and down, she was so excited.

"Yeah, and get this, Beverley is sneaking out to the gig toneet, she's banned by her mum after her nearly drowning when Cain messed her about before."

I said, "Ruby, she didn't nearly drown, she just sat in the river and got her dress wet and then went to bed for a fortnight."

Ruby tutted. "You've got no imagination, you. Come down and see the owlets wi'me."

I said, "I can't, the girls are coming round soon to get ready."

"Good, I'll come round and get ready as well."

"Ruby, you aren't going to the gig."

"I am."

"I heard your dad say that you're too young."

Ruby kicked a stump.

"If me mam was still here, she would let me go. It's only because he's a bloke and he dun't know owt."

I'd never asked Ruby about where her mum was and I didn't want to ask her now with my hair in curlers and the curry powder making my eyes water.

She stomped off down to the barn.

The girls arrived just after lunch with their stuff for the gig.

They hadn't managed to find out much else about the taxman–Dother Hall situation because all the teachers were away and Bob was left in charge. And he was locked in his studio.

Jo was beside herself . . . but not about the downfall of Dother Hall. About the phone call from Phil. She said, "What time is it? Should we go to the phone box now and sort of stake it out, so that no one else can go in at seven o'clock?"

To distract her, I said, "Let's start getting ready. You'll want to look your best for the phone call." To my amazement, she thought that was a good idea.

The girls have brought their clothes and makeup in

little cases. And we started doing pre-makeup moisturizing. Honey said to me, "Tallulah, there ith brown thtuff in your eyebwow . . ."

The rest of them moved away from me.

I said, "It's only curry powder."

Flossie said, "That's what they all say."

I washed it off.

Honey knows a lot of tips about makeup. She said, "The thing ith to enhance your natuwal beauty, not cover it up."

So for instance, because Flossie had "such a nice fwinge" she should make more of her lips. But not bother with her eyebrows because it was pointless. To enhance my green eyes, Honey showed me how to do layers of mascara and then said eyeliner would weally set them off.

I'm going to miss her when she goes, she's so confident and nice. Like when she looked into Charlie's eyes and she didn't start doing Irish dancing or blinking her eyes like a fool.

I am going to try and be more like her.

At six thirty we were all ready and Jo was bouncing round like a bean on jumping bean powder. Even though it was only early evening, it was pitch-black as we made our way over to the gig. There were lights streaming out of the hall and we could see people inside unrolling cables and setting up a bar. When we got nearer, we heard guitars being tuned up and already outside there were figures sloping around in the shadows.

Vaisey said, "I think I can hear Jack on the drums. I wonder if he knows I'm going to be here. He said 'see you at the gig,' didn't he? But that might mean 'see you all at the gig' but he didn't say 'see you *all* at the gig everybody,' did he?"

We shook our heads.

"If . . . if he talks to me, you don't think the Bottomly sisters will get me, do you? I mean, he's not a village lad, is he? He's just in the band, but maybe they think that's like being an honorary village lad?"

Was there really going to be trouble? Who knows? Who cares? I am not interested in any of the village lads anyway. And never will be.

Quite a few of the other girls from Dother Hall started arriving as well, primping around with compacts and lipsticks and giggling. They are all excited about The Jones. They think they are cool. Hmmm, well, they have never had their noses licked by any of them. Milly and Tilly were both dressed exactly the same.

I said to Jo, "I think that is a bit on the weird side, myself. They are not twins. In fact, even if I was a twin and my twin was wearing orange culottes, I wouldn't feel I had to. Anyway, I think orange culottes are just the kind of thing to annoy the Bottomly sisters."

Jo said, "Is it seven o'clock yet?"

I don't think she has heard a thing anyone has said for about four hours, she is so wound up about Phil's phone call.

The five of us went over to the telephone box at about quarter to seven and stood around waiting. It was all a bit tense.

Jo kept saying, "What shall I say? What will he say? Why is he calling? Is he calling me because he doesn't want to see me again? Why would he call to say that? I wouldn't call to say that, would you?"

On and on.

Honey said, "Welax. Bweathe. Think 'I am in my glor-wee. I am gorguth. I have got a twemendous bottom.'"

We were so nervous that even though we'd been waiting for the phone to ring when it did we all screamed with fright. Jo stared at the ringing telephone like a demented rabbit and I had to get her by the shoulders and put her next to the phone. And pick it up for her.

We stood a little way off to give her some privacy.

Flossie said, "What's her face doing?"

I looked. "I think she's shouting."

Oh dear.

Ruby came out of the darkness with Matilda. Matilda was still wearing her tutu although I noticed it was a bit grubby and had almost come off at the back.

Ruby said, "What's Jo doing?"

I said, "She's shouting."

Ruby said, "Oh, bloody hell, I hope she doesn't vandalize the phone box."

As we waited like telephone guard dogs, more and more people were turning up at the hall and queuing to go in. It was mostly locals but no sign of the Bottomlys. One or two of the village girls looked at us but they didn't smile.

Then Jo slammed down the phone and came out of the phone box. She looked like thunder.

Oh nooooo.

We went up to her and gave her a group hug. And she started sobbing. Oh crikey.

Then she yelled, "Get off me, you losers!!!! He likes me, he likes me, he really, really likes me. AND he's got a plan. He's got a plan!!!"

We all started whooping.

Vaisey said, "What is it? What is his plan? Is he going to be good and ask to come back to Woolfe Academy?"

Jo said, "No, he is going to do something SOOOOO bad that he will get sent back to Woolfe Academy in disgrace by his very disappointed parents!! Yes!"

I said, "What sort of thing is he thinking of?"

Jo said, "I don't know, he thought at first he might burn the school caretaker's shed down with Bunsen burners but he thought that might get him sent to Borstal. It has to be something bad, but not criminal."

Vaisey said, "He could tie all the teachers' shoelaces

together so they fall over."

Flossie said, "He could kidnap the headmaster and then just send bits of his clothes to the school. You know, like a bit of his tie, or the toe from one of his socks. With a ransom note saying, 'Let Phil go back to Woolfe, otherwise the trousers get it!'"

She really has gone mad.

I think she and Seth Hinchcliff may be a marriage made in heaven (ish).

He's a rusty heathen crow

By the time we stopped talking about Phil and what he could do, the joint was quite literally hopping inside and out. Vaisey was so wound up about seeing Jack that she was practically herding us into the hall like a collie dog. Ruby snuck in with us but one of the blokes from The Iron Pies who was on bouncer duty saw her and said, "Ay up, Ruby, I see thee, you little madam. Get along home now, your dad'll have our guts for garters if we let thee in."

Ruby was livid and was kicking the wall.

I said, "Never mind, Rubes, your day will come. We'll go and see the owlets tomorrow and you can wear the lipstick I bought you."

She just said, "Huh."

Then one of the village lads ran into Ruby's legs on his bike. I think they call him "Bites yer legs." I asked

Ruby why and she said because he was called Norman. And I had said, "Oh, I see," but I don't. He was about Ruby's age.

She clattered him across his head and he said, "Ay up, Ruby, going my way, luv?"

Ruby looked at him. "What, with thee?"

He said, "Aye, I've got some tripe for the dog and I've got summat for thee as well. Interested?"

Ruby said, "Might be."

He said, "This is my offer, tripe for tha dog and I'll bike you home and give thee a snog if you're lucky."

Ruby hit him over the head again. Which seemed to me the right thing to do, but then she said, "All right, shift up."

And she got on the back of Norm's bike. Matilda trotted off behind, her little doggie bottom waggling under the pink tutu.

This place never ceases to amaze me. You never read stuff like this in *Jane Eyre*. I don't think the Brontë sisters would be on the school curriculum if people really knew what the North was like.

Inside the village hall, the stage was set up with microphones and a drum kit. Vaisey said, going a bit redder, "That's Jack's kit, I think he's got new sticks."

One of the big lads that I'd seen at The Blind Pig

was doing a disco before The Jones came on. Quite a few peeps were dancing around and Flossie said, "Let's cheer ourselves up by doing the famous Hiddly Diddly Diddly dance as a group. None of us have got the knees for it, besides Tallulah, but we can do our best."

I felt proud that I had a dance named after me and when the next fast record came on we all started leaping and waggling our legs. It made you a bit hysterical leaping up and down. My knees were coming into their own. I was leaping higher and higher!! Vaisey's hair had gone mad.

As we did our grand final leap, the music stopped, and the Bottomly sisters arrived. We were panting and leaning against chairs. And Eccles, Chas, and Dil came and looked at us. I mean really came and looked at us. Looming over us with their arms crossed.

It's not just Beverley that's got big arms; it's all the Bottomly girls.

Eccles said, "Look at the state of you lot, tha's'll never get any decent lads to look at you."

Dil said, "Not unless they were gormless lads from the Funny Farm."

And they all laughed. Then Eccles said, straight to me, "Ay, and you long lanky streak of nowt, keep your bloody hands off Cain. I'm watching thee."

And then they went off to talk to some lads by the bar.

Eccles really has got an enormous bottom.

I said to the girls, "I wouldn't like to get involved with her bottom on a dark night."

After a few minutes of looking at who was there (what I mean is noticing that Charlie *wasn't* there) the disco stopped and the lights on the stage went dim. Then the big lad from The Blind Pig said into the microphone, "Ladles and jellyspoons, it's what you've been waiting for, so go crazy as I give you our own local lads, the one, the only, The JONES!!!!!!"

Jack came shyly on first and Vaisey started clapping wildly. He looked at her and smiled. He is a sweet-looking boy, and it's nice that he likes Vaisey. Unless he has a funny turn like he did when Cain told him that the band shouldn't have regular girlfriends because it spoiled their image. God, he's vile. Cain, I mean.

Next was Ruben Hinchcliff. He looked very annoyed and he was either wearing a lot of eye makeup or he had a black eye. When Jack sat down at his drums he waved his drumstick at Vaisey and she went all red. Aaaahhhh.

She said in my ear, "He's waving with his new drum-stick."

I wish I had someone to wave at me.

Jack started rocking out on the drums and Ruben joined in on bass.

Then Seth Hinchcliff swaggered on. He had his guitar

slung around his waist like a gunslinger. The girls went, "Oooohhhhh," and Flossie said, "Oh yes, he's the one for me."

I looked at her. "Flossie, they are like wild animals in trousers, as I've said before, you . . ."

But she was smiling at him from underneath her fringe. And he caught her eye and winked at her. This is bad.

This will only end in tears.

And I wasn't the only one who thought it was bad. The Bottomly sisters had noticed the looking thing between Flossie and Seth, and they were looking over at us. Uh-oh. We huddled closer together.

Then, after a long pause, Cain Hinchcliff, the Black Prince himself, strutted onto the stage. He looked at us, then turned his back, lit a fag, and stubbed it out. Then lit another one.

I whispered, "You see what he did. People don't count stubbing cigarettes out as littering, but it is just the same thing, you know I—"

Flossie said, "Be quiet, Lullah. I am looking at Seth."

The crowd was chanting, "The Jones, The Jones, The Jones!"

Cain turned around and picked up the microphone. He growled into it. "Why should I bother wi' thee?"

Someone at the back shouted, "Coz we luv thee lads."

Cain snarled, "Love? What's that all about then? ALL LOVE IS PAIN!!!!"

And the music started crashing out as Cain shouted over the top of it.

He was snarling, "Your love is my pain!!!"

Kicking the amps and glaring at the audience.

Bloody hell. I wouldn't say he knew how to have a nice time. He's always so cross. And the lyrics are not exactly happy and cheerful. Flossie said, "I don't think their mummy and daddy told them that they were little sunbeams for Jesus."

Near the end of the first set my ears were buzzing. The crowd was clapping and yelling but then Cain spoke softly into the microphone, "Keep it down, lads." And Jack, Seth, and Ruben began playing softly. Cain went on, "This is a special song for a lass I know . . . very well. If tha knows what I mean."

There was a restless sigh through the crowd. Knowing Cain, probably every girl in the village thought it was a song for her. At that moment Beverley entered through the side door. Cain saw her and said, "This is a song for someone, someone who knows who she is."

Beverley looked like she was blushing and smiled at her sisters, who did a thumbs-up to her.

The lyrics to the song were:

I thought you were off, but you're not
Tha just keep hanging around

Like a bloodhound
I've already got a dog.

As soon as she heard it, Beverley flung off out of the door and the other Bottomly sisters bustled their way through the crowd, saying, "Beverley, luv, hang on! Dun't go near that river! He's not worth it."

At the end of the set, we went outside for some air and sat on the wall.

Vaisey said, "Jack's quite good at drumming, isn't he?"

I said, "Well, he can certainly hit things."

A few of the boys from Woolfe were strolling in. Ben was there and as he flopped past me he smiled.

Then Honey said, "Hello, Ben, you look weally handthome."

I was sort of hoping that Charlie would turn up. But there was no sign of him.

Jo was in seventh heaven. Going on about Phil. "He said he really, really wanted to get back to see me. He likes me, he likes me, he really, really likes me. You were right about the human glue thing, Lullah. He mentioned my cracking snogging. Ooooh, I wonder what he is going to do to get back to Woolfe Academy? It's la romantic, isn't it?"

She really thinks I know something about human glue. Which I don't. So far I've had a bat kiss, then a nice kiss that turned out to be from a boy who just wanted to be my mate, and finally a nose-licking incident.

I wish I had someone who would mention my cracking snogging. I wondered if Charlie had liked snogging me at all? Maybe he hasn't got a girlfriend and he only pretended to have one because I was so useless at it.

It's so unfair, how can you get good at snogging if no one will give you a chance?

We were sitting on the wall in the moonlight when Seth wandered out. He had a towel and was rubbing at his hair as he leaned against the side of the door. All cocky and relaxed. Rubbing his hair. The Hinchcliffs have got twisty mouths just made for sneering and saying mean things. They are quite handsome, I suppose, if you like that sort of dark maniac look.

He stared at Flossie, who got out her compact and put some lippy on. Then she snapped the compact shut and stared back at him.

Seth said, "Nice."

I looked at him haughtily and sniffed and he looked at me but just at my front bit, so I put my arms across my corkers. I hope I am wrong about them growing three inches a week otherwise they'll be able to be seen over Grimbottom.

To change the subject and ignore Seth, I said to Vaisey, "Ted Barraclough has started a band. It's called The Iron Pies. Ruby said that they are going to be doing local gigs."

But she wasn't listening to me, she was too busy smiling at Jack who had also just come out.

Jack said shyly, "Hello, Vaisey. How is it going, all right?"

Vaisey blushed and bobbed her curls around. "Yes, yes . . . We're all very much enjoying your playing. Are you liking your new sticks?"

Jack said, "Yeah, did you notice? They're special ones I got in London and they make the hard hat really ping out."

Hard hat? Ping? Vaisey was nodding her curls about, and the next thing I knew, she and Jack had gone off "to look around."

Seth shouted after them, "Don't do owt I wouldn't do, Jack. And that leaves you a wide field. You little sinhound."

Then he said to Flossie, "All right, big lass?"

Flossie adjusted her glasses. Then she went over to him and looked him straight in the eyes. He put some chewing gum in his mouth and chewed on it and then said, "Cor."

Flossie slapped him on the back quite hard and said, "All right, big lad?"

He choked on his chuddie but as she turned away, he slapped her on her bottom. Jo and I stood closer together. Like the sheep. Now he'd done it.

Flossie stopped and turned round. They were nose to nose, and for a minute we thought she was going to kiss him. Noooooo, she must have gone mad. But then just as he was puckering up, she slapped him hard on his bum.

He shot into the air and said, "Bloody hell. You've got a firm hand for a lass, tha might have ruined my singing career."

As we went back into the gig, he said, "Grrrr."

And she snarled back, "Grrr."

I said to her, "What on earth are you doing?"

And she said, "Growling."

I said, "Why?"

And she said, "I don't know. I've got youthful high spirits. He brings out the animal in me."

Vaisey came in just before the gig began again. Her hair looked like mad hair and she was all blushy. Flossie said, "What have you been up to?"

Vaisey said, "Well, you know, we, well, Jack was all excited about, well, his sticks and everything, you know."

Jo said, "Never mind about his sticks, what kind of snogging did you do?"

Vaisey looked even redder.

"Well, we . . . He held my . . ."

We all shouted, "WHAT??? Your what??"

I said, "Your corkers, did he hold your corkers? Your bottom, was it your bottom?"

Vaisey said, "No, of course not. He held my hand—"

Jo said, "Aaaah, that's sweet, he held your hand. How lovely and romantic, holding your hand."

Vaisey said, "No, no, he held, well, he held my handbag. In case it was . . . heavy."

Crikey. I couldn't think of anything to say.

There was no sign of Honey. I wondered where she was?

Oooh, there she was, over by the bar talking to Ben.

He looked like she had hypnotized him.

The Bottomlys came back into the hall. They were with a big crowd of village girls, gathered round Beverley near the edge of the stage. Beverley looked like she had been crying. Eccles put her arm around Beverley's shoulders and glared at us.

Why, what had we done?

Eccles was chewing on something (possibly cow heel) and said loudly, "Dun't take no notice of these posh twits and dun't take no notice of 'im, he's a bad un, Beverley, all of them Hinchcliffs are."

Beverley was snuffling. But she's got quite a loud voice so we could hear what she was saying. "He said that I was allus moaning on and that he wanted his freedom."

Eccles said, "Well, give him his bloody freedom then, let him sling his hook."

Then the lights dimmed and the big lad from The Blind Pig leapt onstage and said, "Once again, it's them, they're back. Our very own local boys made good. Well all right, maybe not good, there's been the odd feighting but here they are, they're loud, they're proud, they are . . .

The Jones!!!!!" Jack came on (yes, with his new sticks) and started doing a drum roll, and Ruben came on and took a bow, then Seth, who spat out his chewing gum and took up his guitar. And last Cain ambled on.

He said, "Are you still here?"

I thought he was talking to the audience but realized he was looking straight at Beverley.

He started singing a low really menacing song.

I said to the girls, "Is he singing 'Put your coat on, girl, you're leaving'?"

They nodded.

And he was singing it directly to Beverley. She was dabbing at her eyes with a handkerchief.

She looked at him and he looked back and then still singing, he went to the edge of the stage and brought on a coat. It was Beverley's coat that she had on when she came in. He threw it off the stage at her. She caught it and the crowd went, "Oooohh," although a boy did call out, "Well held, that big lass!!!" and Beverley rushed sobbing out of the hall.

Hell's teeth, he was a cad.

I despised him.

Even if Beverley didn't like me, I don't think he should be so mean to her.

When The Jones finished, people clapped and cheered. But not the Bottomlys. And not me. I folded my arms. Cain saw me and gave me his twisty smile.

And I gave him my very worst look.

That would teach him.

Folded arms and a worst look.

Then he did this thing, in front of everyone. In the spotlight. He looked straight at me and he put his tongue out and did a licking motion.

Oh my God.

He was doing licking off the hailstone.

The Bottomly sisters turned round. Dil rolled back her sleeves. Her arms are huge.

Flossie said, "I don't know what that was about, but as Cain said, put your coats on, girls, we're leaving."

And that's what we did.

We walked away from the gig all linked up. And as we looked back, Eccles, Dil, and Chas were standing in the doorway of the village hall. Eccles put two fingers to her eyes and then pointed them at us.

Honey said, "I don't think they weally like us, those village girls. One of those wough village boyth bought me a dwink and a girl looked at me in a howwid way. Like thith."

And Honey screwed her face up and wrinkled her nose.

I said, "That is definitely not a liking type of face. In fact it looks like Matilda's face. It wasn't Matilda in a frock, was it?"

We walked to where the path to Dother Hall started,

and there was no sign of us being followed. Flossie started her Southern belle shenanigans again. "Why, I am sooooooo pooped with the goddam heat an all."

I said, "It's beginning to sleet."

Flossie gave me a casual slap on the back of my head and went on. "And those young men, all gathering around . . . That Seth boy just a-bothering me with his sly ways."

I said to Honey, "What were you doing with bat boy?"

Honey said, "He's quite thweet weally. I was just giving him a bit of twaining."

We all looked at her.

Flossie said, "What do you mean, twaining?"

Honey said, "Well, itth like Wuby thaid, thome boyth don't know how to do thingth and tho you have to teach them. I didn't have much time, but I took him outthide . . ."

I said, "Is that what you were doing? He looked like he'd been hypnotized."

Honey said, "Yeth, I used my eyeth on him."

"Cor," I said. "You did hypnotic eyes?"

Honey fluttered her eyelashes and said, "Oh yeth. And then I taught him about tongueth tho that he doesn't do the bat thing again."

I said, "Did you tell him that I said kissing him was like having a little bat trapped in my mouth?"

Honey shook her golden hair about. "No, thilly, boyth

like to know how to be good at thingth. I told him, 'I will teach you about kithing pwoperly tho that girlth will like you.'"

As they went up the path to Dother Hall I could still hear Jo's voice echoing amongst the trees.

"Phil likes me, he really, really likes me. He—"

Then Flossie's voice, "Miss Jo, will you stoooop that goddam racket before you force me to do something that ah will regret."

Jo shouted, "No!"

There was the sound of a struggle and muffled shouting.

And Vaisey saying, "Flossie, she'll stretch your cardigan with her head if you don't let go."

And finally Flossie singing, "I'm just a girl who cain't say nooooo, I'm in a terrible fix!"

As their voices faded off, I walked slowly across the green.

It was a full moon and the lights were still on in The Blind Pig. I wonder where Alex is. In his room somewhere in Liverpool.

In his frilly shirt. His frilly nighttime shirt. I'm sure he doesn't wear pajamas. He's not a pajama sort of guy, I think.

It would have been nice to have seen him.

Although not when Cain was doing his licking thing.

I wouldn't have liked to have to tell him about me being ice-cream girl.

Alex would never lick a girl's nose. Unless it's something I don't know about yet. Maybe "nose-licking" is on the snogging scale somewhere. I wish I'd written the bloody thing down now. Maybe "knee-hugging" is on there as well, in which case I've been snogged by the lunatic twins as well as everything else.

In my room, I hurried into my jammies because it was cold and snuggled into my bed. I put my hand under my pillow and got out my Darkly Demanding Damson Diary.

There was Alex's letter at the back. I opened it again. Mmmmmmmm.

Three kisses, you wouldn't put three kisses to a mate, would you?

I wonder if Alex ever thinks about me?

He sent me a note so he must remember me. You wouldn't write a note to someone you didn't even remember, that would be stupid. If I was like Honey and good at kissing and fluttering my eyelashes and making my eyes hypnotic perhaps he would like me more. Hmmmmm.

I lay in bed listening to all the scurrying and shrieking outside. It was either wild pigs or the Bottomly sisters.

Just before I switched my light off I wrote a note for myself in my Darkly Demanding Damson Diary.

Practice Hypnotic Eyes.

And even though I didn't mean to, I also wrote:

Ask Honey if I can practice more snogging on the back of her leg before she goes to Hollywood.

She is off to Hollywood on Tuesday. I wonder who she will snog there? Will the American snogging scale be the same as ours?

I bet even they don't have a number for nose-licking—Eskimos might though.

The ladder of showbiz

ON MONDAY MORNING, AS I went through the big front doors in my welligogs and hung my coat up in the cloakroom, there were loads of girls surging around as usual. I don't want to leave here. If Dother Hall closes, I will never climb the ladder of showbiz and wear the golden slippers of success. It will be welligogs all the way for me or maybe even lace-ups.

Milly and Tilly came up to me as I took my coat off and said, "What do you think, Lullah? Why did Cain do it?"

And Milly said, "Why did Cain do that weird thing to you? You know, the licking thing? The village girls were all hufty with us after you'd gone. Ecclesiastica gave us a message for you. She said, 'Tell your gangly posh mate I know where she lives.'"

Oh goodie, what was going to come first: being chucked off the ladder of showbiz or having the golden slippers of applause stuffed up my nose by Eccles?

Then Lav and Dav came sauntering along.

Lavinia smiled her superior smile and said, "Hellll-looo, Oirish, did you have a naaaice weekend, to be sure, to be sure. We all went down to London town to see a show, didn't we, Dav, it was railly something. Kevin Spacey was in it as Richard the Second and he was, like, simply amazing. Railly, you know, lived the character. Amazing. His hump was, like . . . so alive."

I couldn't think of anything to say about a live hump, so I nodded and made for the loos.

But she kept on walking alongside me.

"What did you do, Oirish, did you do some of your special dahnsing to the village boys' band??"

And she and Dav laughed. She put her arm around me and squeezed my shoulder and said, "Just joshing, Oirish, what did you do?"

I said, "We danced and, you know, chatted and . . ."

She said, "Ooohhh, have you been talking to boys, have you now? Any fella you've got your eye on? One of those naughty The Jones boys, is it? Or—no, I bet it's one of those lads from Woolfe."

What did she know? Had someone told her something? Had one of the boys from Woolfe said, "Charlie snogged Tallulah, and she was useless at it"? Maybe Charlie had told Jack and he'd told bat Ben and all of Woolfe Academy knew.

But Lav just said, "Was, er, Alex around at the dance at all? I've got a great idea for *A Midsummer Night's Dream*—it's a sound poem with gongs."

I said, "What do the gongs do?"

And she laughed.

"Oooh, Tallulah, begorrah, begorrah." And pinched my cheeks and said, "Keep smiling."

I wish she would take her imaginary hands off Mr. Dream Boy. And off me.

Everyone was worried about what was going to happen to Dother Hall.

Jo said, "What if Phil does manage to get himself back to Woolfe and then I get sent home?"

And Vaisey said, "Jack may never carry my handbag again."

It was all so sad. Flossie said that Sidone and Monty and the rest of the staff had been away over the weekend and got back very late on Sunday and that Bob had been in charge.

Vaisey said, "He was in his studio playing loud rock music. When he came out he said, 'This is a bum rap, like when Iron Butterfly split, the pain was enormous.'"

I wonder what had been going on. Was there a plan

to save Dother Hall?

I soooo hope so.

We went into assembly and for once everyone was talking quietly.

We fell silent as Sidone walked onto the stage, followed by Monty, Blaise Fox, and Dr. Lightowler. Gudrun came on last, with what looked like a roll of wallpaper.

I said to Vaisey, "Now is not the time for decorating."

Sidone was dressed in sports casual. She was wearing jogging trousers and an England shirt. Her hair was poking out of a cap that had a visor but no top that Americans often wear and I don't really know why. Perhaps their heads are hotter than ours because of global warming.

Sidone started speaking very clearly and loudly, "Girls. Last Thursday, known as Black Thursday, we were in a state of despair. Our feet were bleeding, our hearts were leaking tears, and tiny sobs were cascading from our souls."

She came forward to the lip of the stage, then she paused. She held her fist in front of her.

"But we rally. We carry on. Because . . ."

And she burst into song.

"'There's no people like show people, we smile when we are down . . .'"

She started swaying, so did Monty. As she sang, we all

started swaying. Swaying was catching.

"'Everything about us is appealing, everything the censor will allow . . .'"

At the end she waved her hand at Gudrun.

Gudrun didn't notice at first because she was sniffling and swaying so much, then said, "Oh yes, good yes, it's me, oh yes, rightio."

And tripped over a chair leg. Then she staggered on with the enormous roll of wallpaper and taped it to the back wall.

It said in big red letters:

We shall not, we shall not be moved!

Everyone went, "Hip, hip, hurray!!! For she's a jolly good fellow . . ." and Flossie started a sing-along version of "Sailing, we are sailing!!!"

Sidone waited for quiet.

"The thing is, my girls, we must go on—not just for us, not just for the showbiz world but for our own community. They need us in Heckmondwhite. In Skipley. In Blubberhouses."

We looked at each other. Yes, I think we had a good idea of how we were needed in Heckmondwhite and Skipley and Blubberhouses. And at The Blind Pig.

Sidone went on. "I want all of you to think of spreading the word: Save Dother Hall. Some of you could entertain the shoppers in Skipley with songs. Or a mime piece on the village green? Clowns juggling with tinned produce in the post office. Think of the fun, girls. Get your thinking caps on. Mr. de Courcy has a splendid idea for market day that he wants to show us."

Monty smiled and walked offstage. He was taking off his favorite tweed jacket and undoing the buttons on his trousers. I said to the girls, "Mary Mother of God, he's not going to do a fund-raising stripathon, is he? The village lads will tear him apart."

Jo said, "It's not a bad idea. He won't get any money for taking his clothes off but I bet a load of people would give him money to put them back on!" And we sniggered.

Sidone said, "I am sure you will have many bright ideas of your own, my little stars. And Mr. Barraclough at The Blind Pig will be more than happy to have a performance in his pub."

Monty hove back into view. In his dance tights. He began tap-dancing and singing to "If you go down to the woods today you're sure of a big surprise."

Oh holy angel Gabriel and all his cohort!

As we filed out, Flossie said to me, "Yes, Tallulah, do you remember what larks we had, when we last performed at The Blind Pig? When you were a little horsie and you were so good, weren't you, that Mr. Barraclough still offers you apples."

* * *

At home time, Flossie, Vaisey, Jo, and I pretended we were popping down to Heckmondwhite to get some good-bye jammy dodgers whilst Honey packed. But we had the jammy dodgers already! We were really making up a tribute song to Honey in the music studio.

After about half an hour of practice, Flossie said, "Er, Lullah, I'm not being mean or anything, but can you just play the tambourine?"

Walking home, I was talking to myself to keep warm.

"So, in conclusion, I have accidentally got into a performing arts college, hooray, and then just as I was chugging along on the showbiz express of life it has crashed into an unexpected otter. Boo. But there is a plan, to get the showbiz express back on track. Hooray! And do you know what that is? We're going to improvise *A Midsummer Night's Dream* in The Blind Pig, in tights, and go into the village and let the village folk laugh at us in our tights. And the Bottomly sisters and the village girls who already hate us will have a field day hating us and laughing at us in our tights.

"Then as a coup d'état Alex will turn up and see me in my tights and that will be the end of my life. And then Dother Hall will be closed down anyway."

Oh noooooo. Boooooo.

Good-bye to a Tree Sister

IT MUST BE SOMETHING to do with the harsh weather conditions but I have woken up with Northern grit. I may wear a short-sleeved T-shirt today. I wrote in my Darkly Demanding Damson Diary:

Even though all the fund-raising plans are mad, at least we're doing something. We're fighting back. We're fighting for our slippers.

All right I can't sing or act or dance or—well anything—but maybe I can do an owl-based performance. Yes, yes, I can train Lullah and Ruby to do something. A "guess how much poo an owlet can poo in ten minutes" competition.

Or I could put different hats or wigs on them as famous historical figures.

The hats would have to be little. A little pirate's hat or a Cleopatra wig. Dibdobs could knit them.

Or Matilda could tap-dance on a tin tray. I could make the tappy noises with castanets. That should make a few quid before she fell off the tray.

More ideas later.

I'm going to pop down to see the owlets after school for inspiration, and I'll call for my fun-sized mate Ruby. Connie, the mother owl, will be out night hunting. I hope. I definitely don't want a repeat of what happened when Alex came with me to see them, and Connie swooped down unexpectedly from the barn roof. And I leapt onto Alex's back. Like a mad turtle shell.

Hang on a minute. Actually, perhaps I do want a repeat incident of that.

Me on his back. Mmmmmmm Alex.

Me and Alex. The turtle and his shell.

And anyway, when he next sees me, he will find me greatly changed. Changed in a way that makes him think, "Yum yum." Rather than, "Crikey, I've got a shell on my back."

I'm going to write down what might happen when we next meet.

I will be sitting on a tree felled by lightning. Wearing my new winter shorts with new three-quarter over-the-knee socks, reading a book of poetry.

It is by me.

Reading aloud my latest poem.

On nights like these, I am like a ripe fruit, ready to be plucked.
A peach, a perfect proud peach, a polished purple plum,
A naughty nectarine, a darkly demanding damson . . . a fat fig.

No, no, not a fat fig. A tall tangerine? Hmmmm.

I am lost to the world. Unaware I am being observed.

My long, black, silky hair tumbles softly, flicked by the prevailing North wind.

Alex watches from the trees, in his frilly shirt and breeches. Then a rude, coarse, red-faced man huffs into view.

It is Ted Barraclough. He says to me in his coarse voice, "This bloody wind is from Russia, the Russkies do it on purpose to spoil my curry nights on Fridays. They know that folk won't turn out when there's a cold wind blowing. And stop flicking your hair about, you daft lad."

But I think he talks rubbish.

I don't think Ted Barraclough even knows which direction Russia is in.

Crude, coarse Ted leaves and it is then that I notice Alex crouching in the undergrowth.

I am struck dumb by the sudden surging of old familiar feelings.

I know he is at his fine, fancy theater college, but I see he is still wearing the breeches I know so well.

His flouncy white shirt open to the waist.

He runs to me and takes me in his arms. I close my eyes, it is too much, I am melting, I am melting, and he says softly, "Hello. We is here, wiv our bumbums out."

I opened my bedroom door.

There they were, the mad twins, naked from the waist down.

Looking at me.

Oh goodie.

I can't believe that Honey is actually leaving. Because of all the Dother Hall business, I haven't really thought about it properly. The Hollywood people are sending a car to pick her up and take her to the airport today!

How can you kiss the back of someone's leg and then they just leave? I suppose people might call it calf love. (That's one for my diary.)

I've written her a good-bye letter. With a proper ink pen and some paper that Harold made. It's got pressed flowers embedded in it so it looks special. It says:

Dear Honey,

I am so sad you're going away to the City of the Angels or Los Angeles as some people call it who have no art and theater in their veins. It will suit you to live in the City of Angels because of your golden hair and your honey-ness.

Anyway, I just wanted to say I will never forget you, and perhaps when I do my world-famous Irish dancing tour, I will get to visit you in your luxury beach apartment. Because I just know you are going to the tippy top of the toppermost. You were always going to be a star, but also you are one of the nicest girls I have ever met.

And a true pal.

Good-bye, Honey,

I promise I will keep up all you taught me about my inner glowee and be proud of my knees.

P.S. And thank you for the snogging-the-back-of-the-legs lessons.

I have learned a lot. Now I just need some boys to practice on.

I remember what you said about not being too darty tongued.

And I am going to do that hypnotic eyes

thing that you do.

I've tried it out in my head and it works a treat on me. I'd follow me anywhere.

Lots and lots and lots of love,

Tallulah

Your friend.

P.P.S. There are blotches where my tears have dropped onto the paper. It isn't snot.

I struggled up the lane toward Dother Hall in a near-gale-force wind with the rain lashing down. It's pointless having an umbrella. You might as well hold a piece of jelly in front of you. It's turned inside out about fifty-eight times. Brrr and also grrrr. Just when you think the weather can't get any more Northern it does. It surprises me that people here haven't got webbed feet. In fact, I am pretty sure the Bottomly sisters have.

The weather matches my mood.

In assembly Sidone was dressed in black velvet and a veil.

She said, "The day has come, my girls, when one of our brightest stars goes to shine in another universe. Today Honey leaves us for Hollywood and sometimes only music really says what we can't say. So her friends have put together a song for her. Vaisey, Jo, Flossie, and Tallulah . . ."

She beckoned us to the stage. This was our chance to show the school what Honey meant to us.

Flossie started on her own in her deep voice, slowly.

Honey, Honey,
Oh, Honey, Honey

Then Vaisey joined in with her lovely sweet voice.

You are our lovely girl
And we can't help loving you

Then Jo joined in.

We can't believe the loveliness of little you
We just can't believe you're true

And as the tempo built, it was my turn. I gave it my all, banging on the tambourine as the girls sang.

Oh, Honey, HONEY
SWEET LITTLE HONEY
YOU ARE OUR LOVELY GIRL
and we can't help loving yooooooooooooooooou
Honey, oooh, Honey, OOOH, HONEY
HONEY!!!

As a finale, I flung the tambourine high in the air. Sadly I missed it on the way back down and it struck

Dr. Lightowler a glancing blow to the head.

Afterward as we trooped out everyone was applauding and quite a few people were crying. But as I passed Dr. Lightowler she said, "You complete and utter idiot."

I gave my little letter to Honey and we hugged. I didn't even mind our corkers touching, who cares if I'm a lezzie. Whatever that is.

Honey said, "I'll wead it on the plane, Lullah."

Vaisey was sniffling and said, "Let's go to our special tree and have a last dance together."

We tramped through the damp woods, feeling damp and sad.

I said, "I bet it was like this when Em Brontë died."

Flossie said, "You certainly know how to make things go with a swing, don't you, Lullah?"

Jo put her arms around us and said, "It's only Hollywood, that's just four hundred miles as the crow flies."

Honey said, "Yeth, but I am going by jumbo jet."

And we all cried.

When we reached our special tree, Honey said, "Come on, girlth, letth thow the twee all our glowee for one latht time!!"

And we went mad. Jo was shaking her bum at the tree yelling, "Look at this beauty!"

I was throwing my knees up at the tree yelling, "I'm

not a nobbly knee-ed fool, I'm a green-eyed minx! Kiss the knees, kiss the knees!!"

As Charlie walked into the clearing.

Oh no.

Oh yes.

I stopped mid–knee waggle.

Honey smiled at him with her melty smile. "Hello, Chawie, you came to thay good-bye."

He smiled back at her and gave her a hug. "I was on my way to Dother Hall to give you—well . . . Me and the lads made you a souvenir to take with you, to remind you of us."

And he handed her a wooden sausage and said, "We made you this in woodwork. It has a teak finish."

Honey said, "I'll weally tweasure it."

He was on the dash but as he passed me, he said softly, "Tallulah, I really need to talk to you. I've been trying to get to the village but I'm on curfew." And he went off.

The Tree Sisters went, "Ooooooh, Charlie!"

The car came to pick Honey up at lunchtime and the whole of Dother Hall was outside to see her off. Monty had gone through a box of Kleenex. Honey had her boots and short skirt on and she had put her hair up. She really did look like a star.

As we stood outside with her luggage, a sleek black

limo swept up the driveway. The driver got out and said, "Good afternoon, madam," to Honey, and put her luggage in the boot.

And the girls went "Oooooohhh." They were all so impressed. I've never met anyone who doesn't like Honey.

Even Bob gave her a hug and said, "Rock on—see you Stateside when I get back to gigging." Whatever that means.

When it was time for her to go, the four of us clung together. All of the Tree Sisters, crying and hugging. Like there was no tomorrow. Which there isn't for our little gang. We've promised to write to each other. But it was really really sad.

As she got into the backseat, Honey said, "Ooooh, thith ith howwible. I am tho thad. Tallulah, pleathe do me your little Irish dance to cheer me up."

I wasn't in the mood and my eyes were all swollen from crying and so I said, "I don't think I want—"

Flossie blew her nose and said in her Southern accent, "Yes, goddam it, Lullah Mae, let's give Miss Honey a good ole traditional Texan send-off. One, two, three, four, and hiddly diddly . . ."

Jo gave me a socking big biff on the arm to encourage me.

And while Vaisey, Flossie, and Jo sang that little-known Irish folk song, "Hiddly Diddly Diddly," I did my best throwing-my-legs-around jigging ever. My legs had a life of their own. I was just bobbling around on top of them.

I kept it up until the car was out of sight.

Then I panted to the others, "Nothing could feel worse than this, losing one of your first proper chums."

And I burst into tears.

As we trooped off to French, Dr. Lightowler tapped me on the shoulder.

"You don't mind making a fool of yourself in public do you, Tallulah Casey? How very interesting. Perhaps there is something you can offer Dother Hall."

Holy moly, what a miserable day. We read through *A Midsummer Night's Dream* in French, I don't know why. Monty said it would add a certain je ne sais quoi to our understanding. But it's hard to read properly when you are snuffling.

Monty had his hankie out and sighed, "Honey would have been so right for Titania. That lovely golden hair, that sweet voice we will never hear again." And he started blubbing.

That set us all off howling.

As I was moping home, Dr. Lightowler appeared at her office door. Had she been looking through the keyhole?

Now what? She beckoned me in with one of her thin bony fingers. Was she going to peck me to death?

I went into her nest—I mean, room—and she fixed me with those unblinking eyes. Sort of poo-colored eyes.

"Tut tut . . . so many girls looooonnnnng to come here to learn the art of theeeeaater, but it is you who are allowed to come here. With your silly legs."

I looked down at my silly legs.

"I have been thinking about you, and I have an excellent way for you to show how very . . . very . . . funny you are."

I said politely, "Well, you know I don't think I would go as far as to say that I was, you know, very funny, but well, Ms. Fox did say that I was a comedy genius and . . ."

Dr. Lightowler said, "Did she indeed? Well, that is good. I too have got a very, very strong sense of humor."

Crumbs.

"Yes, and I have a very funny idea for you, for when we visit The Blind Pig."

And she started laughing.

I left the room in a daze. Bottom. She is casting me as Bottom. A thick donkey called Bottom.

Wait till Ted Barraclough and the rough lads from The Blind Pig find out about this.

Wait till the Bottomly sisters find out.

Oh my God, wait till Dream Boy finds out.

This is truly, truly the worst day of my life.

And I am counting when Cain Hinchcliff caught me rubbing my corkers to make them grow.

And the licking the hailstone off my nose.

I went to The Blind Pig to tell Ruby all about it. Ted Barraclough popped up from behind the bar.

"Ay up, young man, have you been playing football today?"

I said, "No, we . . . er, we don't play football."

He doesn't give up easily. "Would you like an apple? Can I take the opportunity to say how very, very much I am looking forward to you coming to my humble abode again to prat around like twits in tights."

Before he could go on, I said, "Er, is Ruby in yet?"

He said, "No, she's out in the back field with Alex."

Alex?

Oh joy! Perhaps every cloud did indeed have a silver lining. Alex was here!!

Mr. Darcy come to save me.

I walked quickly round the back of the pub. My heart was racing. I couldn't believe he was here. I'd read my letter from him every day and night for nearly a fortnight.

I took a deep breath and walked slowly up the track at the back. Oh oh oh. There he was! Mr. Darcy, standing with his back to me with Ruby. He wasn't wearing breeches. I don't mean he was naked from the waist down. He was wearing jeans, looking toward Grimbottom.

Ruby saw me first and called out, "Lullah!!!"

Then Alex turned round. He smiled his lovely smile. Oh, Mr. Darcy, Mr. Darcy, can I just run my hands through your chestnutty hair . . .

I didn't say that bit out loud.

He said, "Hey, Lullah!! How are you, my little Green Eyes?"

Green Eyes, he called me his little Green Eyes!

Take that, Dr. Lightowler, he didn't call me Bottom, he called me Green Eyes.

He looks further than my knees, unlike some people. There is indeed a silver lining to every black cloud.

When I reached him he gave me a hug. Mmmmmm, nice hugging. I remembered to do hypnotic eyes. Blinking and staring at the same time. I bet he is thinking, She is indeed a darkly damson, a plum ripe for plucking, a . . .

He chucked me under my chin and said, "Aaaah, you look lovely, Lullah, so lovely. You must tell me your news about Dither Hall. But first of all come and meet Candice, she's at college with me."

He stopped hugging me.

Why was he making me meet one of his mates from college?

What was this mate in the field for?

Maybe she'd come to collect mushrooms because she liked them, and as she was a mate of his, he'd said . . .

Then a girl with long blond hair appeared from the field. She had ordinary length legs. He kissed her on the lips.

Every cloud does not have a silver lining. It has another even darker, cloudier lining.

The hamster slippers of life

ONCE AGAIN, BACK IN my squirrel room. Alone with my slippers. They are not golden slippers. They are squirrel-cum-hamster slippers.

It's so dark and miserable outside. And inside come to that.

I wonder what Cousin Georgia would do now? About Alex. She told me that she dyed a piece of her hair blond when she really liked a Sex God–type boy who was older than her. But she used toilet cleaner because her mum wouldn't give her money to get real hair dye. And then the Sex God came round to see her and the blond streak worked because the Sex God kissed her. But then the Sex God ran his hand through her hair and the blond streak snapped off. In his hand. Like a little hamster.

And he was a bit surprised, but he thought it was funny.

And he liked her and snogged her even more because of her quirkiness.

Maybe that is the thing to do, be more quirky. So that Alex will see that I am not just some silly little girl, I am the girl for him.

I don't think I will do the blond streak thing though.

That might be a quirk too far.

Should I wear a cloak?

Hmmm.

Perhaps not. I don't want him to think I'm a lunatic, just a bit interesting.

I need to emphasize my good bits.

He likes my eyes.

Maybe I should wear eye makeup.

I'm going to try it.

I went and got my makeup bag. I put black eyeliner on the top of my lids. Hmmmm, quite nice. It does make your eyes stand out. It's a bit crooked though so I look slightly surprised in one eye.

I'll even it up.

The lines are quite thick but that might be good.

Honey said you had to use a softer shade on the bottom lid.

So maybe a softy, blurry dark purple line underneath my eye and then joining the black line at the corner.

Like so.

Yes. That is good.

I look about ten years older, I think.

I wonder if my corkers are still on the move. I could do some measuring and . . .

There was the sound of shouting from outside my window.

It was a girl's voice. Maybe Beverley Bottomly. Out there. Shouting at me. Tracking me down. When she's finished shouting, she's going to climb up the drainpipe to get me.

She's going to climb up and make me eat my slippers.

No, I mustn't be silly, she would never be able to get up the drainpipe. Her arms are strong enough, it's just that there isn't a drainpipe.

What's going on?

I pulled back the curtain a little bit and peeked out.

I should have known. Where there's shouting, there's Cain. He was leaning against a tree with his boot up against the trunk. And shouting in front of him was Beverley. He'd got his collar up and was patting his dog.

If I just quietly open my window a crack, I will be able to hear what she is saying.

What I hope she's saying is, "If you don't get out of town, my mum is going to shoot you."

I slowly and quietly inched the window open.

Then I could hear properly. Beverley was crying and her voice was all squeaky. "You . . . you . . . treat me like nowt."

Cain snapped, "Beverley, I told thee, I just want a laff, I don't want a bloody moaning lass following me abaht. It's depressing."

Beverley was snuffling. "You said tha luvved me."

Cain laughed. "I did nowt of the kind. Tha said thee loved me and I said, well, don't."

Beverley gulped. "Oh yer bad, you led me on."

Cain laughed again. "I led thee on? Tha came trailing after me."

Beverley said, "I want to kill you. You're bad and mean."

She went over to him and banged her fists on his chest. He just stood there.

Then he said, "Beverley, why dun't tha go home, to tha mum and dad. There's nowt doing here."

Beverley screamed and ran off into the woods.

Bloody hell.

Cain stayed leaning against the tree. Looking down at his boots.

Then without looking up, he said, "So what dust tha think, lanky lass? What do they want? Lasses? Eh? Whativver it is I can't give it to them."

I didn't say anything. How could he know I was there?

Cain said, "Well, are you going to give me your wise advice? Tell me what you've learned at big school."

Ooooh, he was so up himself.

I stood up and opened the window some more.

"I did happen to overhear you as I was writing my . . . diary."

He looked up and leered. "Is that what tha call it 'writing in your diary,' like when you had them reight big socks on your hands and you were . . ."

Oh, how dare he!!!! How dare he??????

He really was an animal.

Alex would never say anything like that.

Cain was kicking at the tree.

I said to him, "At least I don't spend my whole life making people unhappy and . . . and . . . making them leap into rivers."

Cain looked up at me again.

I looked back down at him.

He said, "You should wesh your face. You look like a bloody panda."

Oh, typical.

I said, "Are you capable of ever being nice?"

And I was just about to slam the window down on him when he said, "I am being nice, you daft mare. What I'm saying is, tha dun't need owt on your face. You've got a reight naice wild pretty face."

I blinked.

Was he being nice?

I would certainly write this down for posterity in my Darkly Demanding Damson Diary. "The Black Rusty Crow was very nearly not entirely horrible."

He was kicking at leaves. Then he said, "I know tha thinks I'm a bad un, and mebbe I am, but I've got reasons for not trusting wimmen. Anyway I can't do owt to please 'em. What they want I can't give 'em. I'm a bad lot and that's the end of it."

He did seem truly upset for once.

I tried to think of something to say.

"Well, you're nice to the owlets, sort of. And your dog."

Cain laughed.

"Oh, well, there we are then, the solution. I'll go out with one of the owlets—or me dog."

The idea was so mad that we both started laughing.

He looks completely different when he laughs.

How strange.

Then he said, "Well, I'd best be off. It's way past your bedtime."

Oh yes, he had to spoil it.

I said, "I'm not going to go to bed tonight actually. I often stay up all night if I like. I may be part owl."

Why had I said that?

What did I mean?

He said, "Ooooooo, you bloody rebel. See thee, nobbly knees. Twit twooo."

A naturally cracking kisser

IT'S BEEN A WHOLE week since Honey left and a week since Alex came back. I didn't see him again after the "Candice" kiss thing. I avoided the village until I knew he would have gone back to Liverpool. I've tried to busy myself by joining in at Dother Hall and going to every class. And I nearly joined the Dobbinses' knitting group. But my smiley face has been hiding the tears of a clown.

I didn't tell the Tree Sisters about Alex and Candice. They've all got boys to think about. Flossie wants us to go looking for Seth, but I told her that every time I see the Bottomly sisters they give me the evils.

I wish something would happen. It's like the calm before a storm somehow. Jo is madly plotting with Phil about how he is going to get himself sent back to Woolfe. There's been no sign of Charlie, or any of the others from

Woolfe—so much for Charlie wanting to talk about "stuff." We've been to the tree quite a few times and they've never turned up.

I do love my mates. But I feel lonely. I wonder if anyone, any boy, will ever, ever like me. Maybe they won't and I'll remain on my own forever.

And I'll be found clutching my squirrel/hamster slippers dead in bed.

My squirrel/hamster slippers are my only company.

And my Fevver man, and Mr. Sudsy, whose head has fallen off.

If I wrote a story based on me, I bet it would be even more depressing than *Jane Eyre*—at least Jane had some blind bloke who liked her. I'm going to write a bestselling story about my lonely terrible life in the North.

Right, I have begun my epic tragedy. It's called, *The Daughter of Fang.*

I haven't used my own name.

Morag ate a cup of cold fat for her supper that night. She had been saving it, along with a potato that she had wrestled from a pig when she had first escaped from Fang's lair on Grimbottom.

As she passed a rock pool, she saw her own face reflected in the cold water. She noticed her green eyes staring back at her, surrounded by glossy black hair.

As she looked farther down her reflection, she saw the bumps of womanhood poking the sack she was wearing. "Oh oh," she—

I was interrupted by some pebbles rattling against my windowpane. I pushed up the window and Ruby was jumping up and down on the wall below me. Bobbing around in her bobbly hat. She was shouting, "Guess what, guess what!!!! Guess what's happened. Guess!!! Go on, go on, guesss!!"

I said, "I—"

"Go on, you'll nivver, nivver guess!!!"

"I—"

"Nivver ever in a million squillion years. Nivver!!!!"

"I—"

"Hahahahahahaha, nivver, I told you, I told you."

This was stupid. I stashed away my diary and put my coat and hat on.

I went downstairs and outside. Matilda had a knitted beanie hat on with ear holes, and her ears poking out.

Ruby was still shouting up at my window and dancing around on the wall. "You can't guess, can you!!!! That's because you will nivver guess!!!!"

I got hold of her around her waist and said, "Ruby, TELL me what I will never guess."

She puffed, "Cain Hinchcliff has done it . . . this . . . time. He has dumped Beverley . . . AGAIN and . . . Mrs. Bottomly is . . . after him with . . . a . . . GUN!!!!"

* * *

After Ruby went off for her tea, I was sitting on the wall thinking about the Cain thing. Well, well, well. So life can be fair. Finally he gets what he deserves. You can't just go around licking people's noses and destroying outdoor lavatories without paying the price.

I wonder where he is?

Hiding out in the undergrowth like the animal he is. Maybe he's with Fang up on Grimbottom, in the dog basket of life. Unlikely though since Fang doesn't exist except in Flossie's head. (And in my new bestselling novel about the daughter of Fang.)

There is an enormous moon hanging over Grimbottom. Dibdobs said it is a "hunter's moon" tonight. It's called a hunter's moon because it's big and red. And it gives enough light to hunt by. I wonder if it gives enough light for Mrs. Bottomly to hunt Cain?

Spooky. She might be out there now, stalking him like a dog. The moon is gleaming on a dusting of frost and there is a sparkle on the trees like fairy dust.

It's a night for romance. If you had someone to be romantic with. And all the Tree Sisters have, apart from me.

Flossie says she is going to track Seth Hinchcliff down and use her snogging techniques on him.

And Vaisey is dying to see Jack again. He waved at her when she saw him on his cross-country run. We had to practically resuscitate her, she was so pleased.

And yesterday, Phil sent Jo a note about his latest idea. He is tunneling out of ordinary school. It sounds like that old film, where prisoners in a camp dig a tunnel so that they can get under the fence and out to freedom.

Jo told us, "He's dug about two feet already. And he's only been doing it for two days."

I said, "How many feet is it to the school fence?"

And she said, "I don't know. How many feet is there in half a mile?"

So if he keeps going at this rate he'll be at the fence in about ten years.

I hear a far-off hooting. Probably Connie out hunting. Using the hunter's moon.

I could go and see my little feathery owlet friends. At least they are always glad to see me. Well, they blink a lot.

When I opened the barn door, Lullah and Ruby started cheeping. Ooooooh, they are so sweet. I am going to give them a big cuddle.

But then I remembered what Bob had said yesterday. It was raining in the dorm and when Bob came to adjust the tarpaulin he was wearing a rain hat.

And I innocently said to him, "Bob, where did you get your rain hat, and do they do them in small sizes because I could get some for the owlets when they start going out hunting."

It was like I had suggested slavery for owls.

He said, "That is totally uncool. They are wild creatures and should be left to groove as wild creatures."

I said, "They do groove as wild creatures. I clap when they swivel their heads. I love them."

Bob was really grumpy about it.

"They are not pets. If they start thinking they are human beings, they can never fit in with the owl community."

Maybe he's right, I shouldn't spoil their owliness. Especially as I'm not going to be here for much longer to look after them. Maybe I should try and be more owly myself?

There, this is good. I am bringing out my inner owl, which has been peeking out for some time. I've got my legs tucked up underneath my coat and my hat pulled down and my hair tucked under it. Good, now I will put my hands in my pockets so that my arms look like little wings.

Blimey, it's hard to keep your balance. The owlets are looking at me and cheeping.

Then I nearly fell off my pretend perch because a boy's voice said, "I thought I might find you here."

Oh Jumping Jehosophat and Lawks, it's Charlie.

I tried to stand up but my legs were caught in my coat and I fell backward.

Charlie loomed over me and he was laughing so much he couldn't say anything.

Because my hands were trapped in my pockets, I couldn't even help myself up.

Charlie said, "Lullah, can I, can I, help you up . . . Are you . . . were you pretending to be an owl?"

And then he started laughing again.

I managed to get my legs out and I pulled my hat off. I struggled to my feet. With my luck my hair was probably in the exact shape of a bird's nest. I brushed some of the straw off me and said casually, looking down at my feet, "I was just . . . just . . ."

He said, "Being an owl."

I tried to explain. "Yes—but—Bob said that you can't be, you know, a person, because they won't leave you, they'll think they're human beings and come in your home and want to go to school and get a decent job and so on."

Go to school? What was I thinking?

I wasn't thinking, I was looking down at my feet.

Charlie said, "I called round at your house, but there was no one in, so I thought maybe you would be here. I came to find you, because I wanted to . . ."

I said quickly, "Talk about stuff, I know, well, it's all right, I've already forgotten about the thing that, you know, you said 'can't we forget about it.' Well, I have, whatever it is."

Charlie sighed. "Look, I want to say . . ."

I said, "Oh, you don't need to. I've forgotten about it. Whatever it was."

I was fiddling with my buttons because, to be honest, I felt like crying. Although I haven't much experience, it seems to me that there is only one thing worserer than having someone not wanting to kiss you, and that's for them to explain why they don't want to kiss you.

Charlie said, "Lullah, will you stop fiddling around with your buttons and look at me? I want to see your eyes."

I said, "I don't want to look at you."

He said, "You won't look at me?"

I said, "No, I won't look at you. I don't want to and I'm not going to."

He said, "What, never again?"

I said, "No."

He said, "Are you sure?"

I said, "Yes, I am quite sure, I am never going to look at you again."

There was a bit of a pause and then his face appeared by my feet. He was lying on the floor and looking up at me.

He said, "Wrong."

He gave me such a shock, but it was actually the first time I'd felt like laughing for days.

He said, from upside down, "Please talk to me properly, this is not my best angle."

He got up and I looked at him.

He smiled and said, "That's the girl."

Charlie looked really nice. Oh, well. I'd said that once I had done the icicle thing with him, I'd like to be his friend.

Like we were before the kissy thing happened. Ah, well.

He said, "Look, you shouldn't be upset just because I'm an idiot. I won't be the only idiot boy you meet, believe me. You can practice on me."

I smiled back at him.

He looked me right in the eyes.

"I will always worship the knees, no matter what anyone else says. Give me a flash to show me you forgive me a bit."

I pulled my coat up so he could see my knees in the tights.

He went, "Cor." Then he said, "Look, let me tell you about my girlfriend. We've known each other since we were kids. She's lovely."

I couldn't help myself, I said, "Oh, that's good," but not in an "Oh, that's good" way.

He said, "Shhhhh. Let me finish."

And then he said, "But you're lovely, too."

I said, "Huh."

And he looked at me and said, "And I shouldn't have kissed you. It was all wrong."

Oh great, I knew we would get to this bit.

I blurted out. "I told you, it's not my fault that I don't know how to kiss properly. I've only just learned how to do it. Well, not even now really, but I've been practicing on legs and maybe, if I went on to balloons like Ruby said, I . . ."

Charlie was staring at me.

"You've been practicing on legs?"

I nodded.

"Because you thought I didn't want to kiss you because you were so bad at it?"

I nodded again. And my face felt really hot.

Then he sighed and came over and got hold of me and hugged me to him.

"Oh, Lullah, I'm so sorry. It's nothing to do with that, you crazy Irish person. I just have to sort things out. I have to see how I feel and then be honest with everyone. I thought about you when I went home. A lot."

I said, "But you're with your girlfriend?"

He looked down at his feet.

"She likes me. She's known me for ages. We got our first bikes together. But, well now, I don't, I mean I'm here . . . Look, I feel all mixed up. And I hope you'll forgive me and will be my friend."

I looked up at him. He had the dreamiest eyes. I wanted to be an icicle, but I was sort of in a daze like in *A Midsummer Night's Dream*. Although hopefully I hadn't suddenly grown a donkey's head.

I thought I heard a creak somewhere. But then Charlie put both of his hands on the sides of my face. He said, "Lullah, I like everything about you. I like the way you look and your beautiful eyes. You make me laugh, which is bloody nice in a girl. And, by the way, you are a naturally cracking kisser."

Wow, this was it. A naturally cracking kisser! We have liftoff!!!

I said, "Am I? Really?"

He said, "Yep, really."

Ooooohhhh.

And I knew he was going to kiss me again.

But then he turned my head down and kissed me on my hair.

He breathed deeply and said, "I have to get back, the dogs will be sent out and I'll be on hopping punishment until Christmas. Don't forget me. Be my friend."

And he went out of the barn door.

Crikey. All right, he hadn't said, "Be my girlfriend"—he'd said, "Be my friend"—but he had said a lot of other great things. So, hi diddily diddly diddly diddly!!

I was doing a spot of spontaneous Irish dancing in front of the owlets and singing, "I am a cracking kisser begorrah bejesus be—"

A voice behind me from the inky darkness said, "So tha's a cracking kisser. That's a turn up for t'books."

Bloody Cain.

The black crow.

I could see the tip of his cigarette glowing.

I said, "Why are you always lurking around in the dark?"

Cain said, "P'raps I like it. P'raps I see more in the dark."

I said, "Well, that's because you're always hiding from people who hate you."

He came and stood in front of me.

"Aaah, aye, that's mebbe true."

I said huffily, as I made for the barn door, "Well, good evening."

He looked down and said, "Off you go, Southern lass, back to your pratting around with your posh mates. I only come to say good-bye to the owlets."

Why did he always turn up like a bad penny everywhere I went?

And see things I didn't want him to see.

Back again in my squirrel room, looking out of the window. I was thinking about what Charlie had said. He said he liked everything about me. He liked the way I looked. He said I had nice eyes. He said I made him laugh. He said I was . . . what else?

I'm going to write it down in my Darkly Demanding Damson Diary. Not on the *Daughter of Fang* page. I'm starting an entirely new story. It's going to be called:

The Girl with the Green Eyes

As she lay in her wooden boudoir, the girl with the green eyes thought back over her evening. She laughed softly as she remembered herself as she used to be. A silly girl, fond of dancing but with legs that alarmed small children and dogs.

But now, since Charles had said, "You are a naturally cracking kisser," she had changed and grown less silly.

Hmmmmmmmm.

But if I was such a cracking kisser . . . why didn't he kiss me?

OK, he kissed my hair, but that's not the same thing. I don't remember hair kissing being on Cousin Georgia's snogging list.

Hmmmmmmmm.

Nice, though.

Anyway, I'm glad we are mates again.

I put my diary away under my pillow. Wait until I tell the Tree Sisters this.

I was all snuggly and warm in my bed and happy. Perhaps something nice might come out of this. Maybe we can save Dother Hall and I can put the bad times behind me. And boys might actually like me and want to kiss me.

As I was drifting into sleep, I could hear gunshots.

What fool was out hunting stuff at this time of night?

Then I sat up.

Cain!

Tunneling for his life

NEXT DAY WHEN I was crossing the green to go to Dother Hall, I saw Ruben and Seth sitting on the wall by The Blind Pig. Seth did a wolf whistle when he saw me. Which is unacceptable behavior, so I swished my hair and gave him a dirty look. He winked back at me. Honestly!

Seth shouted, "Ay, tell that big lass, your mate, Flossie, the one who looks like she could flatten some grass. Tell her Seth says how do and tell her I'll wait for her tomorrow neet at t'back of Dither Hall."

I said huffily, "I don't think Florence cares where you hang about at 'neet.'"

Seth and Ruben both went, "Ooooooohhhhh, get you!!!"

Seth said, "Ay, tell Flossie I'll be there abaht seven-ish."

Huh.

Then Ruby and Matilda came tumbling out for school.

Ruben said to her, "Awreet, Ruby?"

Ruby said, "Aye, I'm all right, but where's that daft brother of yours? Has 'e bin shot yet?"

Ruben said, "She'll nivver find Cain."

Seth joined in. "If Cain dun't want to be fand, he'll nivver be fand."

Ruby flounced off to school and so did I.

I couldn't wait to tell the mates about Charlie.

The rest of the Tree Sisters were with Bob and Monty in the music studio all morning so I didn't have a chance to tell them anything. I was on prop-making duties, making fairy wings. Bending chicken wire and covering it with whatever I could find, mostly newspaper. There's hardly anything to work with.

At lunch I told the Tree Sisters what had happened with Charlie.

I said, "Charlie came to see me in the barn."

Jo said, "Oooooh, what was the 'stuff' he wanted to talk about, if you know what I mean?"

Flossie said, "Was it snogging stuff?"

And I said, "Well, yes, in a way. He said he really likes me, but already has a girlfriend and was sorry for being an idiot."

Vaisey said, "Well, it's nice that he really likes you, isn't it? And, you know, let you know that he was sorry."

I said, "I suppose so. But in a way it would be nice just to have someone who liked me and it not be all complicated."

Jo said, "Oh, it's all me me me with you, isn't it, Tallulah? What about me me me!!!"

I said, "What about you? What's the matter with you?"

She folded her arms. "What is the matter with me? What is the matter with me?"

I said, "Well, what is the matter with you?"

Jo said, "I'll tell you what the matter with me is, I've got a boyfriend who is tunneling for his life."

I said, "Well, he's not, is he . . . tunneling for his life, he's—"

But Jo had gone off on one.

"Tunneling for his life and meanwhile suffering the anguish of being underground and undersnogged."

Then as we were going into Monty's theater improv workshop, I told Flossie about Seth.

"I told him that you weren't interested in where he hung out at 'neet.' And that he could stay at the back of Dother Hall for a million squillion years and you still wouldn't be meeting him there."

Flossie was back in Texas. "Hmmm, you are quite

right, Miss Tallulah. Ah'm not a girl who is easy . . ."

So much for the famous Hinchcliff charm!

Flossie went on.

"Yes sirree bob, it will do that young man no damn harm to be kept waitin'. With his cotton-pickin' insolence."

I couldn't wait to see Seth hanging around waiting.

Flossie went on normally.

"I'll go out about quarter past seven."

What???

Monty was in his tracky bums and wearing a headband, I don't know why, as he hasn't really got any hair to keep out of his eyes.

"Now then, girls, today we are looking at the emotion of being 'drunk with love.' The Bard often speaks of this. For instance, when Puck flings the love potion in his victim's eyes. So, let us start with the eyes. Let us do drunken eyes. Let your eyes go."

Flossie looked at me cross-eyed. Everyone else was looking like something from *Night of the Vampire Bats*.

Monty said, "Right, now tongues. Let your tongues loll in your mouths and try to speak. Let your tongue be like a big fat slug in your mouth."

He was lolling his tongue out and saying, "HHEth-thhtgooooorll. Hecthhhooo."

Jo came up to me with her eyes crossed and her tongue

lolling out and said, "Givvtth a thnoooggggg."

Monty wasn't finished, because then we were on to knees.

At last, knees! Something I could shine at.

"Girls, feel like all the muscles in your knees have become useless—let them go so you have mushy knee complex. Try walking around with mushy knees."

I was excellent at mushy knees, in fact, I was the best.

As we left, Monty shouted after us, "Girls, do not drive or operate heavy machinery after doing these exercises."

We had a "Lost and Found Orchestra" lesson in the hall last thing, with Blaise and Bob.

Bob was on keyboards "improvising" around a tune. I think it was "Chitty Chitty Bang Bang" but I can't be sure.

Blaise shouted, "Girls, find something to make a noise with. A bit of pipe or a comb or a milk bottle. Or use your own body parts!"

Some girls got stuff from the kitchen or garden, kettles and bottles and even a saw.

Vaisey found a creaky door and started harmonizing with it. Sort of "creak-creak, la la lah lah lah!!!" in time to Bob's "Chitty Chitty Bang Bang."

Flossie blew her cheeks out and hit them to make popping noises. It was really good, but she looked like a mad goldfish.

Jo was banging her head with a tin tray so I went and sat next to her and started a sort of counter-rhythm. She banged her head and I did *bang-bang-bang* on the wooden panels on the front of the stage. But I got a bit carried away and put my foot through the wooden paneling.

Bob had to get under the stage and take my shoe off so I could get my leg out. There's a foot-shaped hole in the paneling now.

Blaise said, "We'll have to find a way to keep those legs under control. They have a life of their own, Tallulah."

She doesn't need to tell me that. And of course she doesn't know about my cracking snogging techniques either. And by the way, never will.

At home time I was wrapping my scarf around me, when Lavinia pounced.

"Begorrah, begosh, bejesus, Tallulah Casey. To be sure, to be sure, to be sure. How the devil are you?"

I mumbled, "Fine, thank you, just going home."

She put her arm around me. "Now when are we going to get together with that nice Alex?"

I said, "Oh, I see. Oh, he's been back but he's gone again."

She perked up and flicked her hair about.

"Did he . . . did you . . . ask him about coming and helping us?"

I said, "Well, I didn't get a chance really because he was with his girlfriend, Candice."

Lavinia said, "His girlfriend?"

I smiled. "Yep. Candice."

She said, "Did you know he had a girlfriend?"

I said, "No, but Ruby says he met her at college and they have only just started going out."

Why was I telling her this?

She looked thoughtful.

"Oh, I see. Hmmmm. See you later, Tallulah. Probably a bit too busy to do any lunchtime performances this term."

And she went off.

So every cloud does have a silver lining. But it had made me long for Mr. Darcy again.

It was freezing on the way home from Dother Hall and I could hardly move my face. Ruby came scampering to meet me as I passed the post office. She said, "Brr, come and have hot choccy with me."

I said, shivering, "Is your dad in?"

Ruby said, "Nah, he's at band rehearsal. Come on."

I couldn't find out any more from Ruby about Candice. When I said casually, "So how is Alex doing at college? Is he, does he, see Candice a lot? I suppose they go mushrooming quite a lot."

She rolled her eyes at me and said, "Don't even think about it."

So we sipped our choccy and she showed me some of her art from school.

I said, "What's this one?"

And she said, "That's Mrs. Bottomly stalking Cain on the moors."

I said, "Does anyone know where he is?"

Ruby said, "Nah."

I'd noticed it getting quite windy, and the trees rustling and creaking for the last hour, but then it suddenly got much worse. Doors slammed, and the wind moaned, like a ghostie down the chimney in Ruby's bedroom. Oooohhh, it was a bit creepy.

I said to Ruby, "I'd better get home before the pub blows down. I wouldn't like to be Cain out there in this."

Ruby said, "They're tough, those lads. Since their mam left. Well, you've got to be, haven't you. Get on with it, I mean."

I was going to ask what had happened to Ruby's mum, but she started playing with Matilda and I didn't like to.

I said good-bye and went outside. Jeepers creepers, it was wild. I had to hold on to my hat. As I passed the beginning of the path that led up the back road to the moors, I couldn't help thinking about Cain again.

I know he doesn't deserve it, but I am a bit worried

about him. Out there all alone.

In the dark and cold.

He might die out there. Or at least get pneumonia.

And what will he be eating? I wonder if he is having to cook worms for his tea?

Return of Cain the Bad

AS I STOOD LOOKING up the path, I could see the rocks and crags, bleak against the darkening sky. The wind was whistling and howling. There was something creepy and exciting about it. I liked it somehow, I don't know why. It suited my mood, I suppose.

And also what was there to be frightened of? On the moors? Fang was just a silly village story. How could a dog be half-dog half-donkey? If Fang was half-otter half-dog, that would be more likely. And who could be frightened of that? A dog that really liked swimming? That's not very scary.

As I stood there being blown about by the wind, I was still excited about Charlie saying I was a cracking kisser. If it was true, maybe there was a way I could show Alex that I wasn't just a little girl anymore. I pulled my coat about me. I thought I'd go and look at the moors. I went up the back road as far as the low branch. Ruby told me that if you hung upside down on it, it made you happy because all the bad feelings dropped out.

I'm going to try it. I turned upside down on the branch and was swinging by my legs. In the wind. It was quite peaceful as I rocked back and forward.

The sky looked even more dramatic upside down. Then there was a really loud rumble of thunder and a crash of lightning. I got the right way round quickly. The atmosphere had gone all shivery. It must be about to pour down.

And then I felt a presence. There was definitely something alive very near to me. Oh no.

Fang. He might really, really be real. Maybe he can smell teenagers.

I looked into the dark fearfully. I could see a dark shape. Oooooh noooooo.

It wasn't Fang. But it was nearly as bad.

"What's tha doin' hanging abhat here?"

Cain was there, looking at me from underneath his eyelashes. I couldn't see his eyes very well as he had his collar up.

He went on looking.

And I went on looking.

I was so shocked to see him I couldn't speak. I managed to croak out. "Are you . . . well, are you all right? No one knew where you were. And one of the lads said you might have, you know, been dead."

I could see his teeth curving into a bitter smile. He said, "Why, were you worried abaht me? Did you miss me?"

I said, "No, I didn't, well, you know, we didn't know where you were, and Mrs. Bottomly with her gun and everything."

Cain said, "That woman couldn't hit a bloody elephant, even if it had a target painted on it."

I said, "Oh, OK. Well . . . are you, er, coming back into Heckmondwhite?"

He came a bit closer and sat down on the branch where I'd been hanging upside down. Oh God, had he seen me doing that? Thank Jehosophat, I'd got my trousers on.

He was looking down at his feet.

"No, not yet. Ah'll leave it a bit longer, let things quiet dahn."

I said, "Where have you—I mean, have you got a nice cave to stay in?"

He laughed. "I'm not a bloody dog."

I felt a bit stupid.

Then he sighed. "Ay up, I'm sorry, I know tha's being nice. You're a funny one, you, aren't you?"

I sniffed, "Oh yeah, that's me. The funny one. I know you make fun of me and call me stuff."

He looked at me.

"I don't mean to mek fun of thee, it's just my way. Since me mam went, I don't get on with wimmen right well. They're not straight, they allus want summat."

I said, "Well, I don't want summat. I mean, I don't want anything."

He looked at me and I couldn't help looking back. There was something about his dark eyes.

"Oh, I think you do want something. You just don't rightly know what it is."

I was feeling very sort of scared, I don't know why. Maybe because I never know what he's going to do. Poke me with a stick, laugh at me. Lick my nose.

He said, "I mek thee feel funny."

I said, "Hahahahahaha."

He said, "Anyway up, I'd best be off . . . *to my cave.*"

And he laughed and stood up.

"You bloody duck egg, a cave."

I said, "Well, anyway, erm, see you."

I turned to go back down the path.

My legs felt very wobbly.

They had better not do anything unusual.

I didn't hear him going off, but then I hadn't heard him arrive.

Maybe he'd got slippers on. Why would he wear his slippers outside. He didn't seem the slippers kind of . . .

He was still there, because he said softly and seriously, "Lullah, I shouldn't ask thee this, it might cause you trouble, but will you do summat for me."

I turned round.

He walked toward me, quite slowly, and stood right in front of me. He is quite tall. Now I could see his eyes properly in the moonlight. So black. I felt like a mesmerized mouse. He'd better not peck my head off.

Then he said, "I want thee to kiss me."

I was absolutely paralyzed.

He put both his hands on the sides of my face and bent down and kissed me.

At first I thought my head would just fall off.

But when my brain unfroze . . . I liked it.

He put his hands on my waist and they felt warm and strong.

The kissing thing was a combination of softness and hardness. And it wasn't just my mouth. My whole body felt tingly and warm and sort of melty. He stopped kissing me for a minute, and I didn't want him to. I could feel his breath on my face, all warm in the cold night.

He looked me in the eyes, then he half smiled. I could see his teeth sparkling like pearls. He took my face in his hands again and pushed a strand of my hair back, and then bent his face down to mine again. And gave me little gentle kisses on the mouth. Wow. Then just when I thought I might explode or burst into flames, he kissed me really long. And just a little bit of his tongue licked at the inside of my lips.

It was incredible.

I didn't have any sense of time. It might have been hours or minutes, I had no idea.

But I knew I wanted to go on doing it.

Then I heard Ruby shouting in the darkness.

"Matilda, come back, tha daft apporth." And out of the darkness, Matilda came scampering up the path.

Cain stopped kissing me. He whispered softly, "There you are, Miss. That's given tha summat to think about, hasn't it? See thee later."

And his big black dog appeared from nowhere and looked at Matilda, who lay on her back with her legs in the air.

Cain laughed and said, "We're in." They both slipped off into the dark.

When Ruby huffed into view after Matilda and saw me, she said, "What are you doing up there, yer barm pot!"

I told her a bit of the truth. "Well—I came up here because I was worried about Cain. I thought he might be wounded. You know, and . . . the . . . gun thingy . . ."

I was glad she couldn't see my face in the dark because I am sure it would have been purple.

As we went back down the path, she said, "Don't be so daft, he'll be alreet. Mrs. Bottomly couldn't hit an elephant even if it had a target on it."

I started to say, "That's what he sa—"

But stopped myself in time.

* * *

When I got back to Dandelion Cottage, I felt like a woman. Not a girl anymore. I wonder if my corkers had grown because of the excitement? Maybe everyone will know that something has happened to me?

I opened the front door and went into the kitchen. Dibdobs said, "Ooooh, look at Tallulah, boys! What has she been up to? She's been naughty, hasn't she, boys?"

Oh no, she could tell. Are my corkers sticking out through my coat?

"Her hair is all wild from the wind, isn't it?"

Sam and Max came to look up at my head.

Dibdobs was going on.

"She looks like Jane Eyre, doesn't she?"

Sam said, in between sucking on his dodie, "Jane Hair."

I laughed like a maniac and left them to their sucking. And went off to my squirrel room.

Holy Mother of God and all the Saints.

I flung myself on my squirrel bed and touched my lips, I could still feel them tingling. From Cain. Cain of all people!! Black, rusty crow Cain. Nose-licking Cain.

How could I?

He's awful.

Awful.

But maybe he's trying to be good?

In *Jane Eyre* Mr. Rochester is awful, but then he turns

out to be good.

Only after he has been blinded though.

Perhaps Cain is turning into a nicer person because of his troubles.

Like Heathcliff in *Wuthering Heights*. He is horrid and then he meets Cathy and then . . . oh, well, no, actually he is horrid and then he gets more horrid.

I cannot believe that I have kissed Cain. He must have hypnotized me or something. I must NEVER EVER tell anyone about this.

Not even the Tree Sisters . . .

It has to be my shaming secret.

I put in my Darkly Demanding Damson Diary:

On this day of the year of our Lord, a strange and unnatural urge overtook me. I have always wanted Alex the Good but I have accidentally snogged Cain the Bad.

I am so ashamed I may never Irish dance again.

Warming up my Bottom

I WOKE UP FROM a dream where Fang (smoking a pipe) was saying, "Well, which do you want—Mr. Good, Mr. Bad, or Mr. Huggy?"

When I got up, I reread my diary.

I can't have kissed Cain.

Yes, it did happen.

There it is in black and white.

Ten pages away from Labradad.

I have accidentally snogged Cain the Bad.

No one must ever know the thing that did happen. I hid my diary on top of my acorn-legged wardrobe.

* * *

When I got to Dother Hall there was no heating on in half the school.

The Tree Sisters were all huddled together in the common room, in one chair. Jo said, “For warmth.”

Flossie said, “I’ve got my pajamas on underneath my clothes.”

Brrrrrr. Sidone came in, dressed in a big fur coat with a Cossack hat on.

“Girls, girls, this is where the going gets tough. And the tough go and get their coats on, and gather in the woods—round the bonfire that Bob will make out of the potting shed.”

Bob came out of the boiler room with a black head. (I don’t mean he had a spot, I mean his head was black.) I noticed his T-shirt says, *Do I look like a fool?*

The Tree Sisters all looked at him and then we nodded at each other.

Actually, once Bob had managed to make the fire, it was jolly in the woods. There’s a clearing where some trees have been felled and it was cozy sitting there on dry logs. The potting shed was crackling merrily and embers whirled up into the air. We had school blankets round us and were reading bits out from *A Midsummer Night’s Dream*. The only down side is that Dr. Lightowler is here. Looking at me.

Flossie said, "Why does Dr. Lightowler hate you so much?"

I said softly, "I don't know, but I do know that she is keen as anything to see my Bottom."

And we all laughed. But she didn't. Can she hear everything? She can probably hear voles talking.

We are doing the bit in the play where Oberon, the King of the Fairies, and Titania, the Queen of the Fairies, have fallen out so Oberon gets Puck to put a love potion in Titania's eyes. It makes her fall in love with stupid Bottom, who has magically grown a donkey head.

I whispered to Vaisey, "The only good thing is if I've got a donkey's head on, no one can see me. Or know who I am. Especially if I do a French accent."

We were talking about how many pairs of fairy wings we needed and how we could improvise the forest in The Blind Pig, when Dr. Lightowler said, "Of course, because of the . . . er . . . financial climate, girls, we must use our ingenuity for props and costumes. This is the time for artistic license."

Monty was very enthusiastic. He said, "Let's put our thinking caps on, girls. I have some silk scarves I brought back from India. We could use them. Perhaps for wings. Biffo and I visited India last year and we had matching pantaloons specially made. I would be glad to donate them to the cause!! I've not worn them since I was, myself, Titania in a performance in Skegness."

Jo started a chorus of "For he's a jolly good fellow, for he's a jolly good fellow."

Until Dr. Lightowler shouted, "Quiet!"

Then she dropped her bombshell.

"Thank you, thank you indeed, Mr. de Courcy. And I believe you found something else that you had a marvelous idea about."

Monty said, "Oh yes, yes indeed . . . these."

And he got out of his bag a pair of Mickey Mouse ears and put them on his little fat head.

They looked hilarious. He really did look like a big mouse in a suit.

I said to the girls, "Where is the idiot Mickey Mouse in Shakespeare's masterpiece?"

As we were laughing, Monty said, "I got them from Disney World when Biffo and Sprogsy and I—"

Dr. Lightowler interrupted, "And this is the magic of theater, girls! As soon as I saw them, I thought, bingo! We may not have a donkey's head for Bottom, but at least we have some Mickey Mouse ears! I think it will be very funny indeed for Tallulah Casey to play Bottom as a mouse. It will give everyone in The Blind Pig an opportunity to see how very, very funny Tallulah is." And she laughed and laughed.

The Tree Sisters got hold of a hand each and Flossie patted my head.

★ ★ ★

Dr. Lightowler swooped back to Dother Hall for a meeting with Sidone for the rest of the day, so at least I had a few hours of peace.

I still feel weak because of the Cain, erm, thingymajig whatsit. Ooh, I can't even bring myself to think about it, even in the privacy of my own head.

No one must ever, in a million years, find out about Cain.

Never.

Why did he kiss me? He doesn't even like me.

At least Charlie likes me.

I managed to forget about everything to do with boys for the next hour because Blaise Fox came to do movement with us.

She yelled, "Come on, girls, let's be donkeys. I want to see your inner donkeys!"

I didn't know that donkeys wrestled but Flossie's inner donkey did.

At the end, we had a massive Irish donkey dancing competition which I won.

As I was limping off, Blaise said, "Tallulah, as I may have mentioned before—watching you perform is like watching someone setting fire to their own pants. It's quite remarkable. So here's my plan—you're going to do a solo extravaganza. An Irish donkey 'enchantment' dance. It might not save the college but it will make me laugh!"

Oh God.

* * *

Back in the common room, I said to Flossie, "You're not really going to meet Seth tonight, are you?"

She said, "You bet your bottom dollar, Miss Lullabelle. Seth Hinchcliff is mine for the taking."

Vaisey said, "What will you do with him, Flossie?"

Flossie said, "What won't I do with him, Miss Vaisey?"

Vaisey went red.

I went red because I remembered what I had done with Cain. What if he'd told Seth? What if Seth knew? What if Seth told Flossie?

After last bell went, I told the Tree Sisters I was so cold I had to go home to warm up my bottom. The thought of accidentally bumping into Seth made me feel sick.

I walked home quickly through the dark woods.

As I got to the village I saw a group of the village girls coming out of the shop—Eccles was with them. I had to walk past them to get home and they crossed their arms and stared at me.

Then Beverley came out of the shop. She looks like she has been crying for the last year. She pointed her finger at me and said, "Don't think I dun't know about thee, lady."

And they all lumbered off.

How could she know?

* * *

In my squirrel room, I got my diary down. There was Labradad, there was "Daughter of Fang," poems to Alex the Good, there was "The Girl with Green Eyes" and there was "I have always wanted Alex the Good but I have accidentally snogged Cain the Bad."

I can cross it out in my diary, but I can't cross it out from my lips.

I am a Cain kisser.

The fall of Dother Hall

SIDONE WAS LEAVING IN Monty's sidecar when I got to Dother Hall next morning. Monty was on his motorbike in goggles and helmet, and Sidone had dark glasses and a headscarf on.

She shouted and waved as they rode away, "Off to London, girls, my girls, the city of dreams. Let us hope my charms will work and I can create magic for *our* theater of dreams. Wish me luck, my girls, my dear, dear girls!!!"

Sidone has gone to see some of her old theatrical mates to ask if they can do anything to save the school.

I said to Vaisey, "They'd better hurry up, I've just gone to the loo and the loo door fell off in my hand."

Vaisey said, "Flossie's got a love bite on her neck."

I said, "From Seth? That's, that's . . ."

Flossie was nodding and showed me her neck.

I said, "That's purple eye shadow, isn't it?"

She said, "Yeah. Looks good, though, doesn't it?"

She really likes Seth. She says he is a laugh.

Flossie said, "Miss Lullabelle, that boy is an ANIMAL, an ANIMAL I tell you!!! He is mean, moody, and magnificent!!!"

Seth?

Magnificent?

Seth?

Vaisey said, "Are you seeing him then? A Hinchcliff?"

Flossie said, "I don't know, we'll see how it goes. See how he shapes up."

And she went off humming. Thank goodness no one had mentioned Cain.

Vaisey said, "Is Cain still missing?"

I looked down at my shoes and grunted.

Vaisey was going on.

"Maybe we should, you know, look for him? Or maybe the boys, you know Jack and so on, well, they could keep an eye out for him, when they do their cross-country hopping."

Jo came running in like a demented retriever. Almost barking.

"Guess what? I had to go to Gudrun's office for a phone call. She said it was my dad. And when I answered it my dad said, 'Give us a snog' down the phone."

And Jo started jumping up and down.

We looked at each other. I know my dad was a Labradad but even he seemed normal in comparison to this.

Vaisey said, "Perhaps your dad didn't say 'snog,' maybe he was saying, you know . . ."

Jo said, "No, no, he was PRETENDING to be my dad."

I said, "Why would he pretend to be your dad, when he was your dad?"

Jo trod on my foot.

"So that he could talk to me!!! So he could tell me something!!! PHIL. He pretended to be my dad!"

We all looked at her.

She punched me on my arm.

"Ask me what he wanted to tell me. Go on."

I opened my mouth to say something and Jo said, "Shut up, shut up talking. He wanted to tell me that he has been chucked out of school again and is on his way back to Wooollllllffffffe. Yarroooo!!!! And he says even if he is manacled to the walls, he'll get to see me. Hurrah!!!"

It turns out that Phil dug his tunnel underneath the rugby pitch, but he made it so shallow that during a rugby match it collapsed and some of the older boys fell into it. And the rugby pitch has to be returfed. At enormous cost to the school . . . so he's been sent back to Woolfe as punishment!

We all hugged each other.

At least three of the Tree Sisters are happy. That just

leaves me. Alone on the ship of life. Paddling around in the shallows.

With no boyfriend. Only dark secrets I can never share.

We had a late rehearsal and as we came out of the studio, Sidone got back from London. She was wearing a long black veil. Monty was wearing a black top hat.

I said, "I don't think this looks good, do you?"

Sidone said to us, "Sometimes even I cannot conjure magic and miracles, girls. I regret to tell you, I have been unable to persuade anyone to back Dother Hall. So therefore, everything depends on the magic of theater. Let us throw ourselves on the loving tenderness of our community. We go to The Blind Pig, girls, to give our all!"

I had a really weird horrible dream last night.

A Midwinter Tights Nightmare.

It was set in The Blind Pig.

Mr. Barraclough was Puck in an all-in-one leather jumpsuit. He had some salted peanuts in a basket and was flinging them into people's eyes, and it made them get off with each other.

I was Bottom and I had my Dumbo head on again. I was blundering around, and then Alex came into the pub and Mr. Barraclough chucked peanuts in his eyes and he fell in love with the bloke next to him at the bar.

It was Cain.

Cain got the hump when Alex tried to kiss him and threatened Alex with a pie. They started fighting. Pies were going everywhere.

Then it all went into slow motion. Everyone was there, laughing at me.

Even Matilda was lying on her back and laughing. In a doggie way.

And the owlets were sitting on the bar, cheeping and laughing at me, their little shoulders jiggling up and down. I heard them say, "What a toooo-wit!"

Then everyone stopped laughing as Mrs. Bottomly came in with a gun.

Cain shouted, "Don't worry, she couldn't hit an elephant unless it had a target painted on it."

And I looked down past my trunk and saw a target.

Painted on me.

I woke up sweating and shivering at dawn.

A Midsummer Tights Dream

AS A COUP DE grâce for my part as Bottom, Dr. Lightowler has found some furry leggings for me to wear. She said "found" them. But I wouldn't be surprised if she had "found" them and ordered them from a special magazine called *How to Make Someone Look Like an Idiot*.

I can't believe I am actually going to be in The Blind Pig in front of Ted Barraclough and the rough village lads, in leggings and Mickey Mouse ears. Like a comedy owl.

But I am.

I was lying on my squirrel bed with my head under the pillows when Dobbins knocked at my door. She said, "Lullah, the boys have got something for you. They've knitted it themselves. Well, I helped a bit, but they held the wool."

Oh Jezebel's Mum, what next?

They all came in. The lunatic twins are almost entirely made out of wool now. Hats, earmuffs, scarves, booties, you name it, Dobbins has knitted it.

She is sooo excited about the show tonight.

She said, "Ooooh, Tallulah I am sooo proud of you—you gorgeous, gorgeous girl. Isn't she gorgeous, boys, shall we hug her?"

Max and Sam came to do knee hugging. Sucking on their dodies. I notice the dodies had knitted covers. As we were in the group hug Dobbins said, "Give Lullah her pressie."

And Sam's mitten came up from beneath my waist. He said, a bit muffled from being buried in my knees, "It's for ooooooo."

And Dobbins said, "Yes, it's for Lullah, and what is it, Max?"

Max said through his dodie, "It's an ARSE."

Dobbins stopped the group hug.

She said, "No, boys, that is the wrong word, what is the right word?"

Sam got a bit cross, "Shhhh, lady!!! It is an arse, an arsey arse!"

It's not a knitted arse. It's a knitted heart. With little hands sticking out of it. Which is quite sweet really. At least someone loves me.

⋆ ⋆ ⋆

At six o'clock I couldn't put it off any longer; it was time to set off for The Blind Pig for the final performance of my life.

As I looked over the green, I could see the lights in the pub twinkling in the windows. And a group of village lads laughing and joking outside. I could also hear the sound of guitars and Mr. Barraclough's voice singing, "I'm the god of hellfire. PIES, I'm gonna . . ."

Ruby came tumbling across to meet me with Matilda. Matilda had her tutu on and some fairy wings. Ruby said, "Oooh, look at you. Show me your furry tights."

I said, "I'd rather not."

Ruby said, "Don't be so daft, you big girl. Everyone's going to see be seeing 'em soon, the pub's packed out. You have to show Northern grit—else they'll eat you alive! Anyway, you can't let me down, I've trained Matilda especially. She knows to run out in her tutu and then lie down for you, so you can do your Enchantment dance."

Oh yes, my "Enchantment dance." Or my "Humiliation dance." Or "Dr. Lightowler's Revenge dance."

Still, I am going to gird my feet for heavy bleeding and hope for the golden slippers of applause. At least Alex the Good is not here to see this.

Bob pulled up in his Bobmobile outside The Blind Pig and the Tree Sisters and the rest of the cast got out.

I walked as slowly as I could to meet my fate.

Dr. Lightowler had her party outfit on, well, her winter cloak. As I arrived, she half smiled. "Aaah, Tallulah, are you excited about your big night as Bottom? I am."

And she swept off.

Why does she hate me?

Blaise Fox came up to me. She said, "Furry tights?"

I opened my coat. She looked me up and down.

"Splendid. Remember, you are not doing this for me, you are not doing it for the school, you are doing it for your inner comedian."

One of the village lads passed by and looked at my legs. Then he said to me, "Bloody hell, what a state. Get the shaving cream out, love."

I said to the Tree Sisters, "It's all right for you. You only have your fairy dance and singing chorus work to do."

Jo said, "Er, Tallulah, I am doing a tap dance with dustbin lids on my feet."

I said, "You've all got your inner thespians to fall back on."

And Flossie said, "Oooooh, well, you've got your cheeky Bottom to fall back on!"

When we went in, we had to squeeze through the bar packed with people and get changed in the ladies' loos. (We knew it was the ladies' because there was a photo of Mr. Barraclough in a dress on the door.)

* * *

Monty's costume is similar to the one he wore when we did the Mummers play, only his tights are green. He said to me, "I've got a little surprise in my codpiece this time that will bring the house down."

We looked at each other.

It was so much worse than I could have imagined.

For a start, the Bottomlys were all there at the front. All chewing gum. Or maybe cow heel.

Sidone came backstage (the loos) and said, "Come on, let's show them our bleeding feet."

We came on as village folk at first, chopping and plucking and hey-nonny-no-ing.

Even Bob had dressed up to play the lute. I don't know if you've heard heavy metal lute playing, but that's what he was doing.

Vaisey, Flossie, and Jo were singing Village People and then Monty came on as narrator. His codpiece got a huge cheer.

He started his improvised hey-nonny-no speech about love. Prancing around with his hands on his hips, pulling scarves from his codpiece. "Gather round and listen to a tale of love. 'Love looks not with the eyes, but with the mind. / And therefore is winged Cupid painted blind.' For love comes in all shapes and forms. Look at yon simple country folk."

Ted Barraclough shouted out, "Ay up, don't be cheeky,

the Bottomlys can't help it."

And that set the tone really.

Lav, Dav, and Noos did their gong song, singing "I'm a fool for love." But repeating "love" like an echo, "I'm a fool for love, love, love, love . . ."

I noticed that none of them had furry leggings or Mickey Mouse ears.

Jo leapt on as Puck and chucked pretend love potion in everyone's eyes, and even the village boys got out of her way. Sidone made a grand guest appearance as Titania. I didn't know that the Queen of Fairies would wear a Dick Whittington costume, but she did.

Sidone sidled up to Mr. Barraclough and put her hand to his face. He began to say, "Madam, I must ask you to be gentle with me. I have an incapacitating pie-eating injury . . ."

But she trilled with laughter and hit him with her knapsack. Then she breathed, "Aaah, such beauty I have rarely seen outside fairy land."

All the village boys cheered.

She went on, panting at Mr. Barraclough, "You strong-thighed son of the soil."

Mr. Barraclough said, "I do my best, love."

All of the pub went "Oohhh."

★ ★ ★

It seemed to be going well, with the pretend snogging and the fighting and Monty's tambourine poetry, but then Puck chucked fairy dust in Sidone's eyes.

It was my turn, to change from Bottom the Weaver into the Donkey-Headed Fool.

Or in my case, the Mickey Mouse–Eared Fool.

I ripped off my peasant's smock and hat to reveal my hairy tights and Mickey Mouse ears. Everyone went mad, which was quite nice actually. Somebody yelled, "Phwoar!"

Sidone came over to me with love in her eyes. She was saying, "Ah me, ah me . . ." And looked me up and down. I did a bit of skipping because it was so spooky. She looked like she might eat me.

Then she said, "Oh, you are gorgeous."

Blimey. Now it was my big moment. My Enchantment dance.

I fiddled with my ears and said, "I know, madam, it's the knees."

And I did a bit of mushy knee walk.

Monty said, "Oh, bravo!"

And there was more applause from the audience. I said to Sidone, "Look at these knees, worship the knees. These knees can make anyone do anything, they are magical knees."

This was the cue for the chorus to sing "Isn't He

Lovely" to an Irish tune.

Ruby waggled a hoofy snack and Matilda toddled out in her tutu and wings. She could see Ruby waggling the hoofy, and lay on her back with her legs sticking up.

Hurrah!

I did my Irish donkey dancing over her upturned legs and got a massive round of applause. Titania swooned.

At the end, as we took our bows, Sidone got up. She walked to the center of the stage and waited for quiet.

"Local community, friends of Dother Hall, girls, my girls. I went to London in an attempt to resolve our little financial misunderstandings, but I am sorry to say that I found myself met on every side by the dark ignorant forces that pit themselves against the artist. Dark ignorant forces who say, 'We are not interested in the ballet—get your wallet out!'"

She swayed and Monty got to his feet. She wasn't going to have to be hauled off like a fish finger again, was she?

She put her head in her hands.

Oh no. Was this the final good-bye to Dother Hall?

She looked at us.

"As you can imagine, I returned to Dother Hall broken. To be greeted by Bob burning the last of the potting-shed shelves . . . and . . ."

Jo said, "I bet our beds are gone."

Sidone hadn't finished.

"Some wonderful, wonderful news!! A letter from Honey's agent in Hollywood, Mr. Bloomfield. He'd heard from Honey about our financial misunderstandings with the creatures who call themselves the Revenue."

She turned to look at Monty and said, "Why they don't just wear black masks and carry bags with *THIEF* written on them . . ."

Monty gave her a hankie and she continued.

"But the good news is, girls, that Mr. Bloomfield has sent us a very generous check!! So, girls, we march on. Limping a little, but carrying on!"

Monty clapped and shouted, "Oh, bravo, bravo."

We all cheered and Flossie said, "Does that mean I can have a bath?"

The Tree Sisters were jumping up and down. I even let Mr. Barraclough wear my ears. Ruby was yelling, "Hurray! Hurray!"

After Sidone's speech, when everyone was hugging each other and Matilda was happily chewing her hoofy, a big black dog came in. It growled menacingly and people backed away from it.

Was it the son of Fang?

The black dog went over to Matilda and snatched the hoofy away from her. Matilda just watched sadly as the black dog took her snack out of the door.

There was a silence, then Mrs. Bottomly shouted, "That were bloody Cain's dog. That black-hearted swine must be around. I'm off for my gun."

I said to Ruby, "Will she really get her gun?"

Ruby said, "Oh yes." And all the Bottomlys stormed out of the pub.

Seth and Ruben came into the bar. They were laughing. Seth clicked his teeth at Flossie, who was still in her fairy costume. "Ay up, big lass, awreet?"

And she clicked back, "Not so bad, big lad."

Then Eccles Bottomly came screeching into the pub again followed by her sisters. She shouted at Seth and Ruben, "Your bloody brother has kicked down our outdoor lavatory again."

Ruben said, "He dun't take kindly to being shot at." And he and Seth laughed.

Then Seth looked straight at me. "Anyway, Cain does as he pleases. Doesn't he, lanky lass?"

What does he know???

Beverley shouted, "He's a bloody animal, he's rotten through and through, you should be shamed to be 'is brothers."

Seth said, "Blood's thicker than lasses."

And he and his brother walked out.

Blood's thicker than lasses?

What does that mean?

Flossie said, "Why that Seth boy, he's gorgeous, isn't he?"

As we surged out of the pub, everyone was chattering. Bob said, "That Honey is a diamond."

It was a clear dark night outside and you could see Grimbottom looming. There was shouting and commotion all over the village and torches flickering everywhere.

Flossie said, "I bet Cain will be back with Fang. Probably having a nourishing Cup-a-Soup."

Will he though?

I shivered. Perhaps he was looking at us even now.

From his black lair.

In his black coat.

As we hovered outside The Blind Pig, inside Mr. Barraclough said loudly into his microphone, "Ladies and gentlespoons, now that the students have finished entertaining us with their lovely version of *Twits in Tights*, it's time for a reight good singsong—may I introduce to you . . . The Iron Pies!" And a loud crashing started. "Pies! Pies, I'm gonna . . ."

Bob was packing stuff into his Bobmobile, but he stopped and said, "Dudes, that is awesome. That is Iron Butterfly reborn." And went back into the pub.

We didn't know what to do after all the excitement.

Flossie said, "Wow, oooh, we get to stay at Dother Hall."

Vaisey said, "I wish I could tell Jack—I thought he might be here."

Jo was chucking sticks around. "When is Phil going to come? Eh? When, when, when? Wheny, when, when???"

Ruby has given us crisps and lemonade so we thought we'd go to the barn and see the owlets before we leave for half term. We crunched down the back path to the barn.

It was nice to get into the warm. The hay and straw kept it snug.

As we sat eating our crisps, I said to Flossie, "You know when you—well—what did you talk to Seth about?"

Flossie looked serious. "Oh, the usual, world peace, the Euro."

Vaisey said, "Really?"

And Flossie said, "No. We said 'hello' and then he snogged me."

We all went, "Ooooooohhhhhh."

I thought Vaisey's eyes were going to fall out. She said, "What was it like?"

And Flossie considered. "Quite nice actually. He's a bit too pokey with his tongue but he improved."

I said aloud accidentally, "Oh yeah, I know what you mean, the tongue thing is tricky, it can be a bit too much like bat boy and not enough like Ca—"

Jumping Jehosophat, I'd nearly said Cain!!!!

At which point, praise be to Our Lady, a miracle happened. Out of the hay burst the Woolfe boys.

First Jack and Ben then behind them Charlie . . . and Phil!

Jo flew off her hay bale and leapt into Phil's arms and they both fell back into the hay. Laughing. And kissing. And fighting. Just like the old days.

It was great to see the boys again. And my little mates, Vaisey and Jo, were so happy. Jo was sitting on Phil's knee, nuzzling his neck and he had his arms around her. He said to her, "Hello, trouble, I'm back!!!" And then they snogged in front of us.

Vaisey and Jack did a lot of big smiling at each other and Flossie fluttered her eyelashes at Ben, saying in her Southern accent, "Why, hello, young fella."

Oh no, she's doing Honey's hypnotic eyes as well. He is putty in her hands, poor thing.

Charlie came and sat next to me.

"Hello, missus."

I said a bit shyly, "Hello."

Charlie smiled and said, "Done any more owl work?"

I smiled back. "No, but I've just been Bottom in mouse's ears and I still managed to do some Irish donkey dancing and mushy knees."

Charlie said, "Praise the knees."

I like Charlie a lot. And I sort of even like him because he told me the truth about his girlfriend. And I think it's nice to know the truth, even if it is a bit painful sometimes.

I told him about the money from Honey's agent, and he told me about Phil coming back to Woolfe Academy and how the headmaster had made him stand in front of the whole school.

Charlie said, "Yep, Hoppy said he'd let his family down, his school down, but most of all he'd let himself down."

I said, "Was Phil upset?"

Charlie said, "Oh yes, indeed. So he set up a gambling club in the dorm."

As the boys were leaving, Charlie said to me quietly, "Lullah, I've thought a lot about you being so worried that you weren't pretty enough or a good enough kisser, and it really upset me. You're top, Tallulah, and don't let anyone tell you any different."

And he gave me a hug.

Then he kissed my cheek.

Then he kissed the other cheek. Then . . .

Phil shouted, "Come on, Charlie, put her down."

Charlie said, "See you next term, gorgeous."

In my squirrel room, on the last night before I leave for Cousin Georgia's for half term. Wow. Just when you think nothing will ever happen, everything happens at once. I'll just add all this to my diary . . .

There was a thud at my window.

I crept over and looked down. I couldn't see anyone there.

I opened my window and looked out.

Then from the dark, a voice said softly, "Ay up, Southern lass—av I woken thee up? I bet I av. I've left summat for thee."

I whispered, "What's that?"

But there was no reply.

I pulled my dressing gown on and crept downstairs quietly, trying not to make the wooden stairs creak. It was pitch-black but I felt around and found Dibdobs's emergency torch by the door. In its knitted torch-holder.

I unlatched the door and crept out in my slippers. The wind was moaning amongst the trees. I pulled my dressing gown tight around me against the bitter cold. The beam of the torch made a pool of light before me.

I went down the side path to just under my window and flashed my torch about. The beam illuminated a knife, stuck into a tree trunk.

Ooooh. This was creepy.

I said, "Cain, Cain, stop this now, it's not funny."

But there was no reply.

I went and looked at the knife. It was stuck through an envelope.

Back in my squirrel bed, with the owls hooting and the wind rattling the windowpane, I opened the envelope.

There, in thick untidy writing, it read:

Love looks not with the eyes, but with the mind
And therefore is winged Cupid painted blind.

Underneath in barely legible handwriting it said:

I know tha likes this sort of thing.
See thee later.

On the train home to Georgia's, I thought, this time I've got something to tell her and the Ace Gang.

I've done nose-licking and other dark things . . . Things that I will never tell another soul about as long as I live.

But I'm not going to think about the bad things, because from now on I will only go for the good.

Like Charlie calling me gorgeous.

And a naturally cracking kisser.

And saying that I was lovely.

Perhaps I just dreamed the dark bits? Perhaps they never really happened.

As the train pulled away from the station, a dark-coated figure was standing by the *Skipley Home of the West Riding Botty* sign.

He turned and winked to me as my carriage passed.

It was Cain.

Tallulah's glossary

barm pot

A fruitcake. If you say, "You barm pot" it's not like saying, "You loonie"; it's more sort of affectionate.

Like saying: "Oooh, you slight idiot."

bejesus

This is from Hiddly Diddly land (Oireland). It's a not-too-naughty swear. Like "Oh my word, you caught me on the knee with that hockey ball."

Or, gadzooks.

Is that any help?

No, I thought not.

Borstal

Is a place for very bad yoof. Like a young person's prison. Woolfe Academy is sort of like Borstal, only the yoof (mostly Charlie, Jack, and Phil) are allowed out now and again to go on cross-country hops.

The hope is that this will make them stop being naughty and get a job in a bank.

This is the hope.

The Brontë sisters

Em, Chazza, and Anne. They lived in Haworth in Yorkshire in . . . er . . . well, a while ago. And they wrote *Wuthering Heights*, *Jane Eyre*, and loads of other stuff about terrible weather conditions and moaning. But in a good way.

corkers

Another word for girls' jiggly bits.

Also known as norkers.

Honkers, etc.

Cousin Georgia calls them "nunga-nungas."

She says because when you pull them out like an elastic band, they go nunga-nunga-nunga.

I will be the last to know whether this is true or not.

corker holders

Something to hold the corkers pert and not too jiggly.

A bra.

Mr. Darcy (and Mrs. Rochester)

Two characters well known for their sense of fun. Not.

Mr. Darcy was in *Pride and Prejudice* and at first he was all snooty and huffy; then he fell in a lake and came out with his shirt all wet. And then we all loved him. In a swoony way.

Mrs. Rochester was Mr. Rochester's secret wife in *Jane Eyre* that he kept in a cupboard upstairs. She was mad as a snake and would only wear her nightie.

In the end it all finished happily because she set fire to the house, went up on the roof for a bit of a dance about, and tripped over her nightie and fell to her death.

Leaving Mr. Rochester blind.

This is one of Em, Chazza, and Anne's more comic novels.

gogglers

Eyes.

To goggle is to look at stuff.

If you couldn't see anything then you would need gogs.

golden slippers of applause

Sidone, the revered and possibly mentally unstable principal of Dother Hall, has her own unique view of the world.

Especially the showbiz world.

In this world she is obsessed by feet.

So her opposite of the "golden slippers of applause" is "the bleeding feet of rejection."

Heathcliff

The "hero" of *Wuthering Heights*. Although no one knows why.

He's mean, moody, and possibly a bit on the pongy side.

Cathy loves him, though. She shows this by viciously

rejecting him and marrying someone else for a laugh. Still, that is true love on the moors for you.

heavens to Betsy

An expression of astonishment like . . .

"Gosh!"

Or, "Crikey!"

Or, as they say in Yorkshire:

"Well, I'll go to the top of our stairs!"

I know it makes little sense but believe me it's best not to argue about these things with Yorkshire folk. Or they will very likely get a cob on.

hiddly diddly diddly

The sound of all Irish songs (and dances). It fits them all. Try it.

human glue

Aaaaah, this is the mysterious thing that happens when two people kiss and there is a sort of "uuuummphhh" moment because they both like it so much. And after that, it's like they have magnetic lips that glue themselves to each other.

I thought that Cousin Georgia had told me about it but actually I think I made it up.

Which probably makes me a genius.

Or an idiot.

laiking around

This means larking about. Or playing.

It sounds quite fun, doesn't it?

But it isn't.

Especially not if it is Cain, the Dark Rusty Crow of Heckmondwhite, who is laiking around.

You don't want Cain to "laik around" with you.

Unless you like ending up sitting in the village stream in your best dress and then having to go to bed crying for two weeks.

lawks-a-mercy

"Crikey" but longer.

lollipop lady

We have ladies who help children cross roads after school. They wear yellow coats and have big sticks with a round disc on the top that says STOP! To stop the cars whilst the children cross the road.

The stick with the round stop thing looks like a lollipop.

If you normally eat six-foot lollipops.

mardy bum

"Mardy" means stroppy. Being a spoiled brat.

You know, stomping around yelling, "It's all about me,

dahling, me!!!! Shut up, everyone, I'm talking!! Look at my lovely shoes! Hurrah, it's me again!!"

Someone who is so bad-tempered and "mardy" that even their bottom is annoyed.

Like Beverley when she found out that although she was engaged to Cain (she bought her own ring), he had two other girlfriends.

Which is why she flung herself in the river.

And ruined her dress because the river was only two inches deep.

Mummers play

Not a mummy's play, which is what I thought at first. Because a mummy's play would be quite dull. People all wrapped up in bandages and dead.

No, centuries ago when people didn't have anything to do and it got dark at three in the afternoon (and that was in summer) they had to make their own "fun."

They had loads of sheep and woad (blue dye) so Ethelred the Unready or someone said, "Lawks it is boring eth what can we do eth? I know eth lettus dye ourselves blue and go eth to ye local pub and bang people over the heads with these sheep bladders. Oh how they will eth laugh. It will be a hoot eth."

And so we have been pretending to be them (the "mummers") for the last 800 years.

nobbliness

I'm on firmer ground here.

Nobbly bits are usually bony bits that look, well, nobbly.

I have loads of it.

In the knee area.

Northern grit

Umph and determination. If you say to a Northern person:

"Don't go out in that storm, you barm pot. The rain is coming down so hard you will be reduced to half your height."

The Northerner would say:

"What rain?"

And go out in his underpants.

plectrum

Surely you know what a plectrum is? How do you pluck your guitars in America? And I know you do pluck a lot of guitars because I've seen old repeats of *Bonanza* and *Dallas*.

But I will explain . . . it's that bit of plastic stuff that you hold in your fingers to stroke the strings so that you don't chip your nail polish.

sjuuuge

When toddlers don't have many teeth (or brains) they can't say words properly. So this means "huge."

Either that or they do know how to say "huge" and are just being annoying.

Maybe toddlers can really secretly talk from birth.

I bet they can read as well.

They are just having a laugh.

And being lazy.

snogging scale

Cousin Georgia has a snogging scale from one to ten.

She told me about it when I visited her last holidays. I think it starts with "holding hands" and goes on getting, you know, more snoggy. Until Number 10, whatever that is. I don't really remember much after "tongues," which I think was 5.

I must ask her to write it down for me when I next see her.

splice the mainbrace

A bit like "Swab the poop deck!"

A nautical term of astonishment.

Like "Shiver my timbers" and "Left hand down a bit."

tannoy

You call this a public address (PA) system apparently.

Which is a very polite term for something which in Yorkshire is a lunatic shouting at you over a loudspeaker on a train.

THE SHOW MUST GO ON!
HERE'S A SNEAK PEEK AT
TALLULAH'S NEXT
(MIS)ADVENTURE:

THE TAMiNG OF THE TiGHTS

Chugging back to Dother Hall

WOOHOOO! AND CHUG-A-LUG-A-DING-DONG. I'M on the train, the celebrity train of life, chugging back to Dother Hall, the theater of dreams. Once more getting ready to fill my Lurex tights! Chasing the golden slippers of success!

I'm prepared to let my feet bleed if necessary. That is what Sidone Beaver, our principal, says we must do if we want to be stars in the theatah dahlings!!! And I for one am willing to fill my tights as much as is humanly possible!!!!

Just call me Tallulah. Tallulah Casey, star of screen, stage, and TV. Well actually that bit is not entirely true—in that I am not a star of the screen. Or stage. Or TV. But I am called Tallulah Casey and here I am back in Brontë country, where Em Brontë—or is it Chaz Brontë? Anyway, one of them wrote the classic *Wuthering Heights*.

Who would have thought that I, a gangly Irish person who had never trod the boards before would be back here for the autumn term at a performing arts college in the heart of the famous Dales of Yorkshire? I am guessing that I'm in Yorkshire because visibility is down to about a foot because of the rain. I think we are stopping at Skipley station. I'll get my case down and hop off.

Uuuumph. Jumping Jehoshaphat and his dad, it's bouncing down. I can just make out the shape of the station sign. Skipley is famous for its otters. I'm not surprised; if this rain keeps up I'll be part otter by Wednesday. Skipley is so proud of its otters that the sign reads *Skipley Home of the West Riding Otter.*

But last time I was here some Yorkshire hooligan had altered the sign so it read: *Skipley Home of the West Riding Botty.*

Honestly . . .

I am squelching across toward it. That's where Cain was standing when I left at the end of last term. The Dark Black Crow of Heckmondwhite. Cain Hinchcliff. Local bad boy made . . . er . . . bad.

I remember him looking at me as the train pulled out. With his dark hair whipping around his face and his dark eyes looking and looking at me. Licking his lips.

He thinks that kind of thing is funny.

I dragged my case along the platform toward the exit by the sign. I hope the sign has been cleaned up since last term because it doesn't give a very good impression of the—

Hang on a minute. The hooligan has been at it again. Now it reads: *Skipley Home of the Brest Riding Otter.*

That is just wrong.

That shouldn't be allowed.

What if American people were on the train? They have a seizure if you say *prat*.

I left the station and trundled across the bridge to the other side, where the buses to Heckmondwhite go from. *Brrr,* I am absolutely soaking. The rain has got in through the front of my coat, and I think into my new bra. Or new corker holder, as me and my new friends say. I hope it doesn't shrink. I might get a corker injury.

Hahahaha. What larks! I am going to put that in my performance-art notebook, my Darkly Demanding Damson Diary. Under "Ideas for modern dance."

As I got to the stop a bus flew round the bend and screeched to a halt. Ahh good, what a relief. The door opened. The warm welcoming bus opening its welcoming doors to welcome me back to my— A cloud of smoke billowed out. The driver was smoking a pipe. Uh-oh. I recognized that balaclava. It was Mrs. Bottomly. She did part-time bus driving as well as cage fighting in Leeds. I got on and pretended to be looking for change in my purse as I said, "Single to Heckmondwhite, please."

Mrs. Bottomly repeated "single to Heckmondwhite, please" in a horrible posh simpering way as she slammed the ticket down. Then she said, looking down at my legs, "Keep those bloody legs off my seats and mind how you go!"

She accelerated away really violently before I had time to sit down and I ended up sitting on the lap of a bloke with a guide dog.

I said, "I'm really sorry but the bus . . ."

He said, "Is it full then, the bus? Is there nowhere else to sit? You're a bloody big lad. My legs'll be numb by the time we get to Heckmondwhite."

At a red traffic light, I staggered to a spare seat.

Everyone on the bus was looking at me and grumbling. I could hear things like, "from that bloody Dither Hall," "simpleton I think," and "They are allus messing about in beards and tights. Sitting on blind people's knees. Bloody daft."

It was raining so hard you could hardly see the road ahead. It didn't make Mrs. Bottomly slow down, though. There was a bump at one stage and I thought I saw a sheep fly past the window but I can't be sure. Then, just as suddenly, it stopped raining, a watery sun came out, and a little rainbow appeared over the top of Grimbottom.

Ooooooh, maybe the rainbow was a sign. A sign that everything was going to be alright. All of my hopes and dreams would come true. I was going to become a star and, more importantly, have a proper boyfriend. Oh and also I might have a corker mini growth spurt! Not just one of them. Both I mean.

When we stopped at my bus stop, Mrs. Bottomly was cleaning her nails with a penknife as I passed her. She didn't look up but she said, "Our Beverley dunt like thee, so that meks me not like thee. Watch your sen, lady. Walls have ears and radishes repeat."

"Thank the Lord the thespians are back!"

I GOT MY CASE down from the bus, and there before me was Heckmondwhite in all its glory!

The autumnal light shining on the bus stop! The village green! The shop! The church! And the pub, The Blind Pig.

My substitute parents the Dobbinses, who I lodge with in term time, are away on a Young Christians Foraging weekend. Harold and Dibdobs and the lunatic twins are nice but possibly the maddest people I have ever met. They are away till tomorrow so I am staying with my little mate Ruby at The Blind Pig for the night. I'm really looking forward to seeing my little pal, and her bulldog, Matilda. Ruby told me that out of eighty breeds given an intelligence test bulldogs come seventy-eighth. But that is the intelligence-o-meter test not the love-o-meter test, which Matilda would definitely win paws down.

What I am not looking forward to is seeing Mr. Barraclough, Ruby's dad. The landlord of the pub and chief tormentor of me and my legs—which have, I must admit, sometimes had a life of their own. When I am nervous or excited they, my legs, well, they initiate Irish dancing. All by themselves. My brain has nothing to do with it. Also because of my skinniness Mr. Barraclough keeps pretending I am a long lanky lad. In a dress.

In a nutshell, Mr. Barraclough and most of the village people think that Dother Hall is for fools. They call it "Dither Hall."

With a bit of luck I will be able to creep up to Ruby's room without Mr. Barraclough hearing me. I went quietly in through the front door of the pub. There is a real racket coming from the bar, so I will just creepy creep up the—

"Well, well, well, thank the Lord the thespians are back!!! I haven't known *what* to do with myself since tha left. By heck is there a giant gene in your family, young man? You've sprung up again, haven't you, lad! What are you practicing being today? Dunt tell me! Let me see." Oh dear. There he was. Ruby's dad. In his leather trousers and Viking helmet. He was looking at me, stroking his chin.

"Hmmm. Green trousers, rain hat, anorak. Big boots. Are you a Hobbit? Is that it?"

I said, "Hello, Mr. Barraclough."

He put his hand to his ear. “Is that elfin you are speaking?”

Just then Bob the technician from Dother Hall emerged from the “Stags” door. He was also wearing a Viking helmet. Over his ponytail. He saw me and said, “Nice one, Tallulah. Great to see you back. Monday I will be there at Dother Hall, the dude with the knowhow, the equipment king, the ‘facilitator’ . . . but tonight I’m the real me. The muso. The rhythm master. Be prepared for total madness. The vibe is going to be like awesome.”

Like awesome?

He went off into the front bar.

I said, “Why is Bob here?”

Mr. Barraclough chucked me under the chin.

“Why is Bob here? Why is Bob here? I’ll tell you why he is here, young man. He’s our new drummer for The Iron Pies. We are going to be a sound sensation. We’ve got our first gig in Cleckheaton next weekend. Good to see you back, young Bilbo.”

He turned into the bar, shouting, “Hit it, lads.”

And an awful din of drums and guitars started up. It really did sound like Bob was just hitting things.

Ruby and Matilda came tumbling down from upstairs. Matilda was leaping up at my legs and Ruby was dancing around me, yelling, “It’s Tallulah lebulla, Matilda. Let’s mek her dance. Do the dance, Tallulah lebulla! Do the dance!!!”

I said with dignity, "I don't want to. You know I have sort of grown out of the Irish dancing thing."

The Iron Pies crashed into their version of a James Bond theme. Ted started singing, "From Russia with PIES I came to yooooooo."

And Ruby had to yell over the top of it.

"Oh, come on just a little bit. For me! I'll sing the Irish song 'Hiddly diddly diddly diddle.'"

So I let myself go. I did my Irish dancing. Ruby joined in and we were leaping and hopping around in the hallway. It was fun actually. There was no one to see me and I needed to let off tension so I let my knees go wherever they pleased.

When I was mid-hiddly I noticed Matilda had got caught in the umbrella stand. Umbrellas were crashing around her. She looked up moonily at us.

Ruby said, "What? What? Why are you mooning me?"

Then Matilda looked at the door and back at Ruby.

Ruby said, "No, I'm not taking you out now. It's time for quiet time."

Matilda started making a snuffling noise, which sounded a bit like crying. Ruby gave in and picked her up.

"Oh bloody hell, alright, Matilda, you daft happorth. Come on, I'll take you out, even though it's going to be a tornado out there. C'mon, Lullah." She rammed a hat and coat on and dragged me outside with her.

Big black clouds were tumbling in again from

Grimbottom and in the distance we could see lightning crackling. Ruby says you can tell how far away the storm is by counting the seconds in between thunder rolls. There was a rumble as we set off up the back path and then another one halfway up the track. We reached the blasted tree with its branch that we used to sit on, and Ruby pulled her jacket round her and shouted above the gathering wind, "It'll start pouring down in abaht five minutes, so go fetch, Matilda!" And Ruby flung a stick for Matilda to chase.

Matilda looked up at Ruby and then lay down like a splayed chicken.

Ruby said, "Oh, you!!! That's not 'go fetch,' is it? That's lying down and dying for England!!!"

Ruby went running off into the bracken waving a stick in front of Matilda, trying to get her to run as well. But I don't think Matilda can run; she can only fast toddle. And she can't do that without falling over. She's not interested in stick fetching. She knows a stick is not a biscuit so why would she want to fetch it? Ruby would have to run along with a biscuit in her hand.

Gosh it was wild up there with the lowering sky and the trees bending in the wind and the moors stretching off. It was getting quite murky and dark and chilly.

I sat down to snuggle in my anorak and put my hood up. I was sitting on the branch that *he* had sat on.

I could feel his warm presence even through my corduroys.

Alex the Good.

I was sitting where Alex the Good had sat.

In a way I was sitting on his knee. If he had been there. On the branch.

Alex. Alex the Good. Ruby's gorgey older brother.

He had gone off to drama college last term but had come back for a visit one weekend. It was late summer and sunny and the moors didn't look malevolent like they did now. He was up here sitting on this very branch and I was so glad to see him again. I had a bit of a crush on him. Even though he probably thought I was just a little schoolgirl, he was always nice to me. Really specially nice to me.

He stood up for me with the Hinchcliff brothers, Seth, Ruben, and the other brother. Whose name I will never mention again. That one.

Alex was always nice to me, encouraging me to fill my tights and to become a thespian. Even when others, like Dr. Lightowler, the drama tutor, failed to see my talent. After my bicycle ballet, Dance of the Sugar Plum Bikey, she said, "Seeing you on stage makes me feel physically sick."

But Alex saw it and he said, "I thought your idea of a ballet on bicycles was marvelous. Anyone could have got their tutu caught in the back wheel and destroyed the backstage area."

Mmmmmm Alex.

Also by Louise Rennison

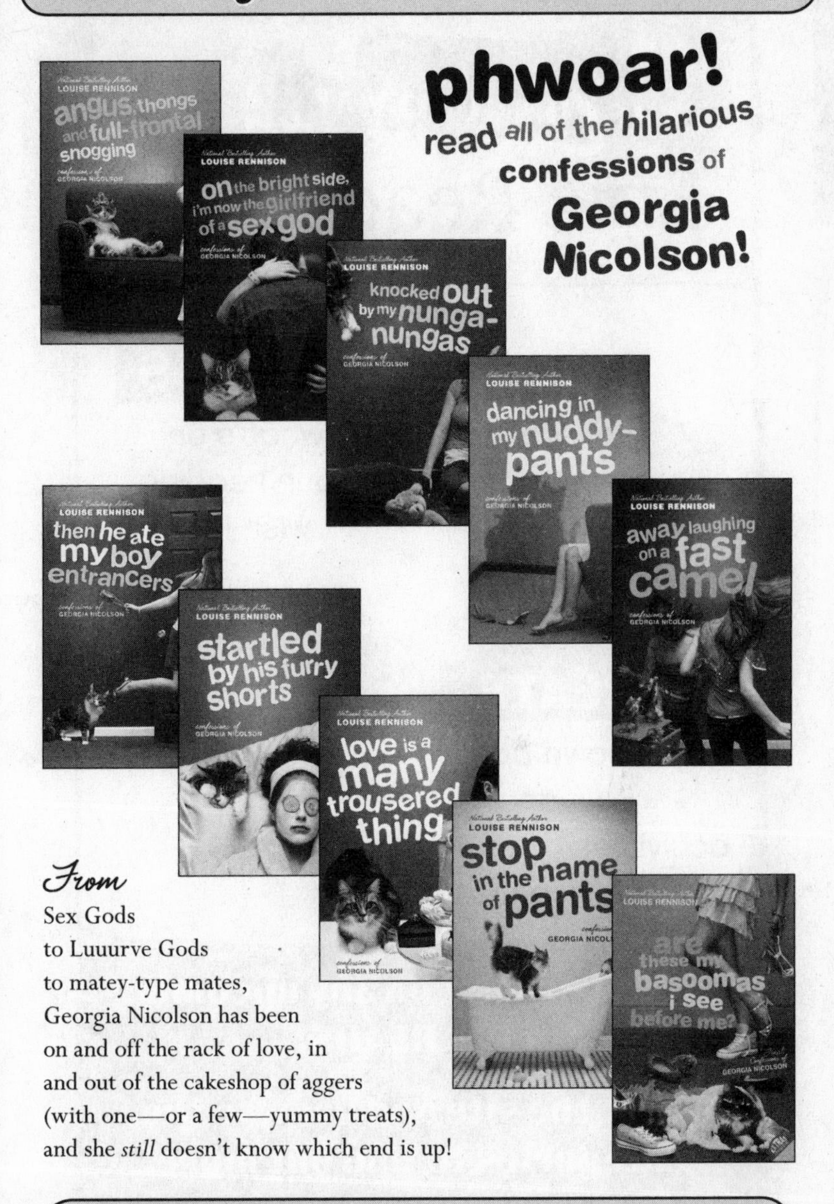

Follow Tallulah's cousin Georgia from the rack of romance to the oven of luuurve in the Confessions of Georgia Nicolson.

HARPER TEEN
An Imprint of HarperCollinsPublishers

www.georgianicolson.com